PING

LISA LUCAS
& STEVE LANDSBERG

HISTORIUM PRESS U.S.A.

First published in Great Britain in 2024 by
The Book Guild Ltd
www.bookguild.co.uk

US – Second Edition in 2025 by
Historium Press
Macon GA 31211
www.historiumpress.com
Email: historiumpublisher@gmail.com

Cover designed by White Rabbit Arts at The Historical Fiction Company
Typeset in 11pt Georgia
Printed and bound in United States by Lightning Source

Visit Lisa Lucas's website at www.lisa-lucas.ca
Visit Steve Landsberg's website at www.historiumpress.com/steven-landsberg

Library of Congress Cataloging-in-Publication Data on file

Hardcover ISBN: 978-1-964700-03-8
Paperback ISBN: 978-1-964700-02-1
E-Book ISBN:978-1-964700-01-4

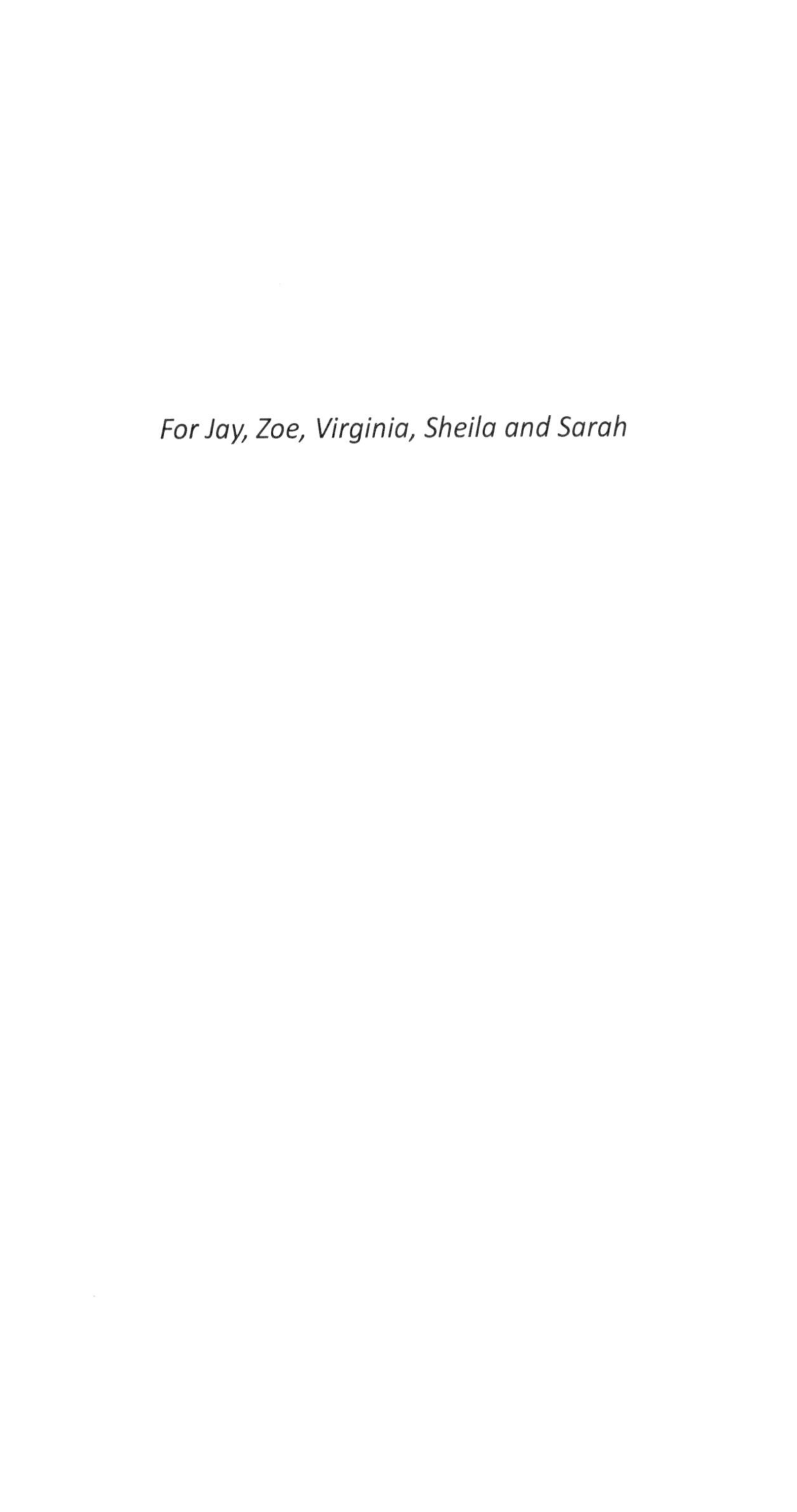

For Jay, Zoe, Virginia, Sheila and Sarah

WARM BUMS
(ENGLAND, 1880)

Table tennis was born in the 1880s as a way to keep the bums of the British upper class warm. When it got too cold to play lawn tennis outside, they brought the game inside and called it table tennis. It was simple. All you needed was a table, a paddle and a little ball.

Over just a few months, the little ball bounced across England where Jacques and Son of London, a sporting equipment manufacturer, kept a close eye on the game's rising popularity and was soon churning out paddles from vellum and cigar boxes and balls out of cork. They didn't worry about the tables. That would come later. For now, any flat surface would do. A list of rules was drawn up and the pieces of the game were neatly packaged. And voilà! Every time a box was shipped and every time a paddle hit the small white ball, pure gold was made.

By the end of the century, tournaments were popping

up across England with hundreds of participants. Journalists filled sports pages with as many facts and figures as they could find about the "new and exciting game". And soon, the little ball made its way across the ocean and into the hands of Parker Brothers, the board game company. Wanting a piece of the action, they acquired the American rights to the name Ping-Pong at great expense and some legal wrangling, and eventually opened a plant with the sole purpose of manufacturing Ping-Pong equipment. The investment paid off.

In less than a decade, the game, once intended to keep upper-class bums warm, grew to become one for all to enjoy. It was fun; the equipment was cheap; and there were almost no barriers to entry. It had become a game for the masses that eventually would find its way to China.

PART ONE

THOSE FUCKING
LITTLE WHITE BALLS

2023

ONE

MATTERS OF FAMILY

Yanking out a chunk of hair from the back of her head made Jenny feel weirdly good. It was almost irresistible – an urge she had never known – an urge she knew she needed to get under control before the bald patches could no longer be hidden.

Hearing her sister's voice down the hall made her want to yank out more but she resisted and yelled instead. "Fuck off, Becca! I'm not going. How many times do I have to say it? I don't give a shit that Grandma is Miss Ping. And I don't give a shit that she's a big deal athlete and I really, really don't give a fuck that Anne Frank played Ping-Pong. So, do you think you can finally shut up about it, Becca?"

Jenny muttered to herself, "It's like Grandma and Anne Frank are gods around here because they played that dumb fucking game."

Slamming the door behind her like a pro, Jenny had

no intention of going to celebrate her grandmother's achievements. She needed a distraction, but when she grabbed her phone and spotted the new post from the posse she despised, she panicked and started feeling for the baby hair around her forehead. One by one, she plucked them out while she thought about how they had followed her onto the court with their phones, waited until she was sweating and her face was all screwed up and then posted all those horrid photos with the caption, *Pretty Jenny, the Queen of Ping-Pong! LOSER!!!*

The thought of it made her pull harder. Each sharp yank giving her a brief reprieve but not for long, so she picked up her phone to finish it off.

"Tell Mom I'm sick of hearing about it. And tell her I can't stand listening to Dad bounce those fucking little white balls on the kitchen table any longer. If he thinks it's cute, it's not. Our whole family has become obsessed with it. It's so fucking annoying! And, Becca, really yell it at her."

Becca's response was simple. "Fuck off! You tell her."

Sitting across from her husband at the kitchen table, Ronnie heard the whole ordeal. She sighed and shook her head in dismay.

"Our daughter's future isn't exactly looking stellar these days. Now she says she can't stand the sound of you, and I quote, 'bounce those fucking little white balls on the kitchen table'. That's a new one. These days, she seems to be focusing all her anger on Mom's event. It's so weird. They used to be so close. I just don't get it." Ronnie looked frustrated and glared at her husband. "Any brilliant ideas, Harry?"

Harry had read his wife's thoughts so many times he knew exactly what to say to avoid another scrap.

"Dr. Salter has told me that now that she's not at school and the bullying has stopped, she needs time to work it through. And working it through won't be easy on her or us. He has seen a lot of this in his practice and thinks it will take time. You need to stop worrying. She'll settle down."

Harry would have usually left it at that, but he was

tired of hearing Ronnie's rants and decided to stir things up. "In fact, he said we should be a little concerned about Becca's lack of pushback."

Ronnie snapped back. "How could Becca possibly rebel? Jenny takes up all the oxygen in this house. God knows, Harry, if you haven't figured that one out by now, maybe you should get your own shrink."

Harry knew he had taken a risk and, predictably, Ronnie reacted. But he felt pleased with himself and momentarily considered grabbing one of "those fucking little white balls" that he spotted on the counter and slamming it on the floor to hear it bounce... bounce... bounce. And while he delighted in listening to the imaginary sound, he also knew it wouldn't be worth it. The house was a tinderbox these days and he didn't know how many fires he was prepared to put out.

Jenny, having heard every word, lay in her bed, madly squeezing the stress ball Dr. Salter had given her to avoid plucking out more hair. She figured she was enough of a freak. She didn't need to be a bald one.

Ronnie tried hard to block out Jenny's rant that was still echoing in her head and focus on what to do next. Somehow, she had to get her daughter to change her mind. This event was important not just for her mother, who was being inducted into the Table Tennis Hall of Fame, but for the whole family. All the arrangements had been made.

Family, friends and sporting officials would be there. And all the invitations had been mailed last month.

Please join us at 4pm on Thursday, May 26, 2023 for

the induction of

Miriam Stahl into the

Table Tennis Hall of Fame.

A true sports hero, her lifetime commitment as an athlete

and leader both on and off the court will be celebrated at

The Cottingham Arena

254 McMaster Drive

Scottsdale, Arizona

TWO

MIRIAM

Miriam had just finished a round of exercise on the mini trampoline she had in the corner of her small living room. She liked to get her knees up and jump at least one hundred times a day. At eighty-four, she felt great. She still played Ping-Pong at the Hills Community Center twice a week and swam at the community pool. She credited her mental strength to Ping-Pong and swimming, to keeping her body strong and to the precious time she got to spend with her granddaughter.

Over the last year, Jenny had offered to drive Miriam to the pool, hang out while Miriam completed her laps and drive her home. It had become her favorite time of the week until recently when the rides had gone silent. Aware of her granddaughter's issues at school and watching her hair thin, she desperately hoped that the silence was temporary. What she couldn't understand was why Jenny kept driving her when she was obviously so miserable? Ronnie had told her about Jenny's refusal

to play Ping-Pong and attend the induction ceremony –
all the stuff that defined Miriam's life and now everything
her granddaughter couldn't stand about her. Maybe the
drives had nothing to do with her. Maybe it was about
that boy she had repeatedly seen Jenny talking to at the
pool.

She was thinking of telling Ronnie that she could
make her own way to the pool and back but figured Jenny
was too precarious and might consider it a rejection – the
last thing her granddaughter needed. Her mood lifted
when the phone rang and she heard Hildi, her younger
sister, laughing on the other end.

"I just found a poem you wrote. It was in a box at the
back of my locker. Do you remember going to that Ping-
Pong picnic and standing up in front of everyone reading
it? You thought you were something else that day. You
insisted on wearing those ridiculous high-waisted pants
and that baggy white shirt that made you look like a man.
And I distinctly remember you telling me that your poem
was, quote unquote, 'amazing'."

Hildi laughed harder. Miriam paused, trying to collect
her memories. Remembering took just a bit longer these
days and it frustrated her.

"No, Hildi, it was a long time ago. What was it again?"

Catching her breath from her laughs, Hildi started to read:

Pingpongitis
Ping-Pong, Ping-Pong,
Such a silly little game,
Play it tipsy,
Play it straight,
The results are all the same.

Boys can play, girls can play,
Nobody gets in a snit,
You can use a brush to bat the ball,
Just have fun,
Keep going,
Don't quit!

So pick up a paddle and a ball,
or even a paintbrush will do,
Just bat it around and jump up and down,
Here's to pinging,
And ponging,
And YOU!

Miriam grinned. Yes, now she remembered the picnic, standing up big and bold in front of her friends who shared her passion for the "silly little game". But Miriam quickly got distracted.

"Okay… okay… it wasn't exactly Shakespeare, but neither am I. What are you doing right now? Can you come over? I need to talk to you. The induction ceremony is coming up and this guy named Marc Gilbert contacted me from a sports marketing company. He told me that he'll be managing the event and insists he needs all the trophies and souvenirs I have 'pronto' as he said."

Miriam paused and took a deep breath.

"He also wants to fly us to Toronto in the next few weeks to the Ping-Pong Summit. Apparently, the organizers would like us to play against one another. They'll put us up for two nights and we'll have most of the day free to tour. To be honest, I think the only reason they're doing it is to put us two old farts on display!"

Both women laughed. But the mood changed when Miriam's voice got serious.

"Hildi, I'm worried about this guy. He's asking me for all the dirt. He thinks it's important that people understand the history of Ping-Pong. As he said, 'the good and the bad and the ugly'. But I was clearly told this event was to be solely about the game of Ping-Pong and my role in it. Why do you think he's asking me to expose what was going on back then? Does he actually think I was involved in the political maneuvering of Nixon and Mao? Is he a moron?"

Hildi sensed her sister's apprehension. "Hold that thought. I'll be there in a bit."

Miriam put down the phone and made a beeline to the kitchen where she gobbled down a chocolate cupcake and a tall glass of whole milk, an emotional crutch she had relied on most of her life when she was stressed. The same crutch that was partly responsible for her struggle with weight and the reason why she wore those high-waisted pants and baggy shirt to the picnic.

Miriam burped, put the glass in the sink and muttered under her breath, "Shit."

THREE

THE POOL

Dimitri took one last toke, threw the joint on the ground and ran to the locker room.

He had to be in the pool by 6:00. The initial shock of cold water quickly dissipated as he began swimming his lengths, a rhythm he had enjoyed in the past but that had recently been ruined by Phil, his new coach, screaming at him on the fucking bullhorn.

"Dimitri, relax your muscles. You look like a bloodthirsty lion ready to pounce. Don't forget to reach as far as you can. Hold on! Stop! Stop! That turn was shit. Let's try it again!"

Dimitri stopped and looked up. He had heard it a million times, but Phil couldn't resist repeating the steps once more.

"Come on! Hurry up! Let's go through the steps again. You need to gain as much momentum as possible when approaching the wall. The faster you go, the better the turn. Don't forget you're doing this blind so use the T at the bottom of the pool as much as you need. I've noticed that you've been zigzagging a bit lately. Don't make that face. It's true, so listen. When you're above the T, and only then, do you begin your half-somersault. Kick like hell and finish by pulling your hands fast and hard directly to your side. I don't think you're pulling down fast enough. You're good at the rest except when you push off the wall, be sure to keep your eyes on the surface of the water. Don't look at your toes. It'll slow you down. I've told you this a hundred times. Okay, let's do twenty."

Dimitri desperately wanted to tell Phil to fuck off but stayed quiet and did as he was told.

"C'mon! We've got to get this right. The meet is next Saturday. You've got one week to perfect your turns."

These days, the only relief from the grueling swim practices was knowing Jenny would be at the pool on Saturdays. He had met her a year ago, shortly after he and his dad had moved to Scottsdale so that Dimitri could train under Phil, a former national team coach and gold medal asshole in Dimitri's mind. His father was determined to get his son, if not on the state team, at least to UCLA on a swimming scholarship, where he had gone.

There were times Dimitri asked himself why he was doing it and why he didn't quit. He was exhausted and wasn't sure he even liked swimming anymore.

But deep down he knew exactly why he kept up the charade. It was Jenny. Although they were "just friends", he often had visions of what it would be like in bed with her.

She was cute, had an amazing body and had a fire in her that was blazing hot. Last month, he saw her take on a young mother who had parked in Jenny's usual spot, designated for the elderly. While Jenny screamed at the young woman and shook her fists, Dimitri enjoyed watching and speculating on how her hot head would translate in bed.

Jenny was interesting in a complicated way, not like the girls he had met at his new school who seemed stamped out by the same panini press. What he liked most was the way he connected with her over what it was like to be an athlete with all the expectations that went along with it – the hours of training that stole so much of their teenage lives. From what Jenny had told him, her life was miserable because of Ping-Pong. Initially, he thought it was a strange sport she had pursued, but after he heard about the family history and what had happened at school, he understood.

Early on in their friendship, Jenny admitted that she drove her grandmother to the pool solely for the extra "bribery bucks" her mother promised her every week, but in the past month, she had stopped saying it.

Dimitri was grateful that Jenny had taken her mother's bribe. He felt that she was the only one who really understood what it meant to be caught in the weeds of a sport that could strangle the life out of you.

FOUR

LOOKING GOOD

Ronnie felt uneasy sitting on the sofa looking past Dr. Salter. She had carefully chosen a tight, black turtleneck and a pair of straight jeans to wear. She knew she looked good... sophisticated and smart. She had arranged this visit after Jenny's ranting had become unbearable. Ronnie felt she needed to get help to understand the complexities of her daughter's behavior and learn some strategies to deal with it. She was banking a lot on this visit. But first, she had to clear her throat. Her fucking turtleneck was strangling her. She coughed but it didn't help.

Dr. Salter grabbed a box of water from his bar fridge. "You okay? This might help."

Ronnie could barely squeeze out enough air to say thanks. After a few gulps, she got control of her breathing, control of herself.

Dr. Salter waited patiently, giving her time to settle.

"In your message, you said that you wanted to talk about Jenny refusing to attend your mother's induction ceremony and how she hates everything to do with Ping-Pong.

"There is a lot to unpack here, and I really shouldn't be talking to you at all since it goes against our professional standards."

Dr. Salter looked straight at Ronnie and paused while he thought about how he could best manage the session.

"But I think it's safe to say this much. As you know, Jenny's life has been intertwined with Ping-Pong from a very young age. She's obviously talented and it certainly sounded like it was a healthy outlet for her. From what she tells me, it all turned to 'fucking shit', her words not mine, when she became the captain of the school team. Getting bullied is hard and what those girls did was nasty and could cause trauma, especially at that age. Unfortunately, Jenny has now decided that Ping-Pong is responsible for her misery, and she therefore wants to cut it out of her life completely. That of course includes your mother. Does that make sense to you?"

Ronnie tensed up at his patronizing question.

"Yes... I get that just fine. But what I don't get is why,

for such a bright girl, she can't distinguish between those horrible bullies and the game itself."

Dr. Salter rearranged himself awkwardly in his chair. "Well, that is more complicated to explain. Let me try. I am hoping that eventually I can get Jenny to actually face the trauma she's experienced in an environment in which she feels completely safe and supported and then have her compartmentalize her thoughts about Ping-Pong so there are no more negative emotions attached to it.

"Best-case scenario would be to get her to a point where she can actually enjoy playing the game again. That way, I'm hopeful she would feel back in control of her life.

"You know, scientists are finding that Ping-Pong enhances brain function unlike any other sport. The fine motor control and eye-hand coordination needed to smack that little ball stimulates the cerebellum and primary cortex. The strategy needed to play the game actually enhances the amygdala which reduces anxiety."

Dr. Salter got up, walked to the bookshelf and slowly picked up a plastic brain that was mounted on a piece of wood. He pointed carefully to the areas he was referring to and repeated the words "cerebellum, primary cortex" and "amygdala" twice. Once the performance was over, he continued to pontificate.

"You know, the overall aerobic exercise required to play not only strengthens our heart function, but it also stimulates the hippocampus which helps long-term memory."

Ronnie was grateful he didn't perform for the "hippocampus" and stayed seated.

"In other words, it's great brain medicine. I'm convinced that if all my patients suffering from anxiety started playing Ping-Pong, I'd have to close my practice."

Dr. Salter chuckled as he swung an imaginary paddle. Ronnie was not amused and decided to steer the conversation exactly how she wanted. After all, she was paying for the session, and she needed answers.

"Well, Dr. Salter, all that brain science sure does sound impressive, but it can't help Jenny now since she can't stand anything to do with the game. Surely, you understand that."

Ronnie was pleased with her jab. It stopped Dr. Salter from talking and gave her time to work through her thoughts.

"Listen, I need Jenny to go to my mother's celebration. It's important not just for my mother but to all of us. What makes this even harder is that since Jenny was very young, she and my mother have enjoyed a special relationship, a deep connection. The two of them have been closer than I've ever been to my mother, and I think poor Becca often feels left out. Frankly, I do."

Ronnie got up and looked out the window. She couldn't stand to look at Dr. Salter any longer and wondered why Jenny thought he was so great.

"My mother taught Jenny how to play Ping-Pong when she was three and since then they've been slamming those little white balls at one another in a way I can't explain. And it's paid off. She's really talented and has won several championships. Trophies lined her shelves until recently when she decided to throw them all in our basement."

Ronnie, feeling emotionally spent, sat back down averting her eyes from Dr. Salter.

"Of course, my mother taught me and Becca how to play too, but somehow it was different. The energy when those two play is electric... you can feel it. You know, Jenny is a strong girl like my mom... until this year when she lost interest in the game. Actually, in almost everything. I blame those damned girls who posted those horrible pictures of her. It was so cruel."

Dr. Salter looked intently at Ronnie as her breathing became shallow and her voice strained.

"Dr. Salter, to be perfectly frank, I get the feeling you're judging me and the last thing I need right now is your judgment. I'm sure Jenny has told you that I pay her to drive my mother to the pool on Saturdays. Yes, I admit, I'm guilty. And I bet you're thinking that I'm a helicopter mama, hovering way too close, and Jenny needs to learn to cope, to be resilient. Yes, I'm guilty of that too. But maybe my daughter can't cope right now. Maybe she can't get past those mean girls. Has that occurred to you?

"I really don't get it. Jenny and my mother were kindred spirits. And now she's refusing to celebrate her – the woman who is partly responsible for changing the modern world as we know it. It's all such a big mess! And you know what? I don't give a shit what you think."

Dr. Salter didn't say a word while he hastily escorted Ronnie out the door.

FIVE

BROKEN

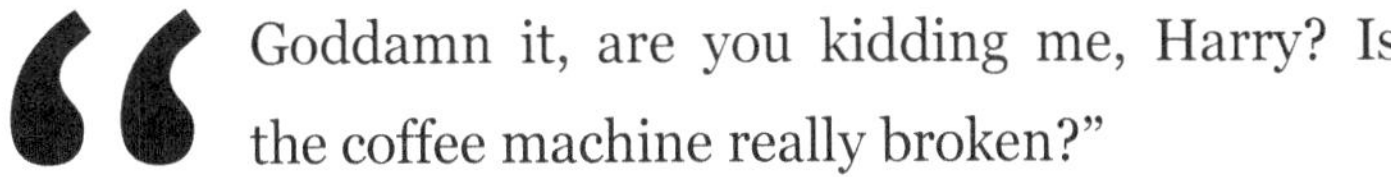

Goddamn it, are you kidding me, Harry? Is the coffee machine really broken?"

Ronnie glared at Harry who had turned the machine upside down to assess the problem and avoid looking at his wife.

"I really need a coffee this morning. I'm exhausted. I was up until 2:00 with Jenny."

Harry watched Ronnie who wasted no time desperately rummaging through the cupboard in search of the coffee plunger to satisfy her caffeine fix.

"Yes, Harry, that's right. While you were sleeping, our daughter was bullied yet again by those girls, this time on TikTok. I hope they ban that fucking platform for good. They posted her playing Ping-Pong again and hurled some nasty insults. I stayed with her while she wailed for hours about how they've targeted her and how she never, ever wants to leave her room again. She finally exhausted herself and went to sleep. It was a bad night."

Harry turned the coffee machine right side up and stared blankly at it. "Should I call Dr. Salter?" Harry asked.

"I don't know, Harry. Last time I met with him he wasn't exactly ready to share any real insights about Jenny. Instead, he gave me a lecture about his professional standards and then presented a little theatrical demonstration on how Ping-Pong is good for our brains."

Ronnie shook her head. "Fuck! At one point, I was convinced he thought he was a Broadway star. I found him patronizing and incredibly annoying. I was determined not to waste the session, but I couldn't wait to get out of there. Jenny says she really likes him, but I don't get it."

Ronnie busily prepared the pressed coffee, took a few sips, paused and took some more. With every gulp, her eyes grew sadder.

"In all her tears, she made it very clear that she has no intention of going to my mother's celebration. She said it's the last thing she wants to do. Harry, she's pushing against everything... absolutely everything."

Ronnie was starting to feel desperate, a feeling she

hated, so she took some deep breaths, lowered her voice and tried to sound somewhat in control.

"I don't know if Dr. Salter is doing her any good. I know one thing. He is certainly providing her with lots of information about anxiety, depression and that fucking trichotillomania. She has at least a dozen pamphlets lying around her room describing each condition and a few others. You don't have to look hard to see how much hair she's pulled out. She won't be able to cover up the bald spots for much longer. Just imagine if those bitches see that! You know, I wonder if all that information is making it worse. Those damned pamphlets."

SIX

THE DAMNED PAMPHLETS

Marc Gilbert arrived early at Miriam's apartment with coffee and bagels in hand and got straight to work. He resented being assigned jobs like this. Managing an old woman who was a big deal during the seventies wasn't exactly why he had gone into sports management.

He took a cursory glance at the trophies and souvenirs lying on the floor and quickly started shoving them into boxes one after another. Miriam cringed watching her life being crammed into 24"x18"x18" folded pieces of cardboard, taped and stacked by the door. She had a sudden urge to tell Marc to cancel everything, but she knew she was in a tough spot. The International Table Tennis Federation was spending a lot of money to showcase her, so she watched, feeling deeply agitated.

"Marc, maybe we should put the trophies in smaller boxes? That way, they're less likely to get damaged."

Marc put his hand up dismissively. Miriam glared at

him. Was he really that obtuse or just dumb? Did it not occur to him that these trophies and souvenirs represented much of her life? Completely unaware of any other thoughts in the room, Marc marched over to the pile of papers lying on the dining room table and started leafing through them. He snickered when he spotted the poem, "Pingpongitis".

"Miriam, this poem is so funny. It's ridiculous. Did you really get up in front of a crowd and read this? We've got to frame it."

Now that he had found one gem, he slowed down and examined the rest carefully. As he scrutinized each piece of her history, he put aside two letters, one from a US senator, William M. Mitchell, and another from John W. Evans, the president of the International Table Tennis Federation in 1971. When he spotted the Time magazine article titled, "The Ping Heard Around the World", he smoothed it out and placed it on top of the pile.

"Actually, there's a lot more here than I expected. I hope the framer I'm using for this job can do it all in time. Don't worry, you'll get it back after the event and then you can hang this stuff wherever you want."

Marc rummaged through his briefcase and handed Miriam a pamphlet.

"You know, I've done a lot of research on you, young lady. You're going to love what I dug up. You really were smack in the middle of the gritty part of Ping-Pong. People are going to eat it up."

On the front was written PING in big, bold underlined letters with a flattering picture of Miriam receiving the trophy for winning the 1947 US Table Tennis Open in Chicago. She smiled. The inside page opened with an article from 1942 when Miriam was kicked off the boys' varsity team. It was followed by one from the Chicago Times about how she was not allowed to participate because she was supposedly using a non-standard paddle that would, according to Janice Baxter, an anti-Semitic team member, give her a slight advantage. The paddles were exactly the same except Miriam had painted her handle blue for fun.

"Isn't it amazing? After this is over, I bet I'll have sporting teams around the world asking me to showcase their players."

Marc laughed.

"And don't forget. We're flying you and Hildi to Toronto next week for the annual Ping-Pong Summit. As I said, all you have to do is play one game. It will be a blast for the audience to watch you girls, at your ripe age, sweat it out! Oh ya, before I forget, they called yesterday and also asked if you'd be willing to do a quick Q&A. I basically said yes. I mean, what do you care, right?"

Miriam dropped down on the sofa. She knew there was no backing out now. She had already signed the agreement to hand over all the relevant materials for the event and, worse, had said yes to be "on display" at the Ping-Pong Summit. Marc looked up and was confused by her reaction.

"Hey, young lady, we talked about this weeks ago. I always said we were going to expose the whole story, even the dirt, and you agreed at the time."

Miriam looked blankly at Marc. Then she fixed her eyes on the boxes Marc had piled by the door, stuffed full of her life of Ping-Pong, her life that was now being used to propel his career.

"Miriam, are you okay? Hey, Miriam, say something. I know, maybe it's not the history you wanted to tell. Maybe I wasn't clear enough when I told you what the mandate was and if so, I apologize. Please say something."

Throughout Marc's life, his blunt manner had gotten

in the way. Miriam's reaction was yet another smacking reminder. But he considered himself too swift and agile to get caught by it yet again, so he walked over and quietly sat down beside her.

"Miriam, Miriam... come on."

And so, Marc, having convinced himself he could bring her around with his boyish charm, playfully poked her shoulder with his index finger.

"Come on, Miriam... ping... ping... ping... ping... ping." Miriam didn't budge.

SEVEN

PING-PONG SUMMIT

The flight from Phoenix to Toronto was delayed three hours. Tired and annoyed by the wait and the idea of being put "on display", Miriam continued to rant about Marc and his asinine behavior. She told Hildi that as soon as they landed, she would call Marc and tell him that they would, as agreed, sit for the Q&A but only under the condition that there were no questions about politics. "It's not my job to tell the young players how politics manipulated the game of Ping-Pong in the seventies and the horrible fallout."

Miriam's voice started to crack.

"Marty would probably still be alive if politics hadn't been involved. Well, Jesus, who knows. He was pretty messed up back then, but for sure the politics didn't help."

Hildi looked at her sister and knew it was time to steer the conversation in another direction before Miriam got herself revved up.

"Miriam, let's fix the game so you win early on. I'll let the ball slip after ten minutes. That's all they'll get from us two old broads. Furthermore, I've arranged to get my hair and make-up done tomorrow morning and I don't want my mascara to run. They won't get to see us sweat. We'll walk off the court looking fresh and dewy, and this Marc jerk can go screw himself."

Miriam smiled thinking how much Hildi still cared about how she looked. How she presented herself to the world really mattered to her. Miriam couldn't give a shit about any of it. Never really did.

The next morning, Hildi got up early to get to her beauty appointments while Miriam ordered room service and watched the news in bed. Listening to CNN's "do-good" report on how China was planning to plant a million trees to clean the air pissed her off.

When Hildi got back to the room, the two women quickly changed into their Ping-Pong uniforms that Marc had sent to the room and walked across the street to the Toronto Convention Centre. It was a huge venue, full of tables with kids and young adults playing. In the center was a table lit up with benches set up for spectators. To the right was a raised platform with a blue curtain behind. They assumed that's where the Q&A would happen. Marc was there, visibly pissed by Miriam's demands but knew well enough to shut up.

The head of the World Table Tennis Championships, Petra Sörling, kept the Q&A light and easy. The questions were focused on their natural talent for the game and how they rose within it. Petra was careful to stay clear of anything controversial after Marc had grabbed her in the hall. She quickly wrote down a new set of questions which hit the sweet spot for the audience and left Miriam believing she had put Marc in his place.

Once their commitments were completed, Miriam and Hildi shook hands with several of the spectators, a skill they had become accustomed to over the years. On the way out, Miriam convinced Hildi to do a quick tour of the exhibit since this year was a retrospective. Hildi reluctantly agreed. As Miriam stared at the photos and grainy videos, she didn't say a word. She didn't need to. She knew the real story of Ping-Pong.

PART TWO

THE PIG

1950-1961

EIGHT

A PIECE OF THE ACTION
(LONDON, 1950)

The Honorable Ivor Montagu could hardly contain his smirk as he finished reading the article, "USA Goes Ping-Pong Crazy" in the London Daily Mail. He laid down the paper that was still warm from being freshly pressed by his manservant, grabbed the sterling silver scissors on his desk and carefully cut out the article.

He put his hands behind his head, leaned back and smiled while his thoughts bounced back and forth between how he had organized the very first tournament as an undergraduate at Cambridge and how much it irked him that the event had been quietly financed by the generous allowance he received from his father. As a communist sympathizer, very few knew about his pedigree – that his family was one of the wealthiest in England, or that Ivor, at four years old, played in the garden at 10 Downing Street while his father met with the prime minister. Just the idea of it made him queasy.

He felt relieved when his thoughts drifted to how he alone had written the official rules and regulations for the game, officially named it table tennis and established the International Table Tennis Federation. Feeling smug, he reveled in the power he had over the game and those who played it, coached it or politically used it to their advantage.

For the few who really knew him, Ping-Pong seemed a curious sport for an aristocrat like Montagu to embrace... a real mismatch. He was, after all, a member of the establishment, of the elite, who should theoretically have no interest in the egalitarian game. Everyone knew it was more suitable to the common man – the hoi polloi.

What they didn't know was Montagu had decided that Ping-Pong was the perfect cover to promote his political agenda. Through it, he could associate and develop relationships with the higher echelons of the socialist and communist governments in Russia and China. His work had nothing to do with promoting sportsmanship and goodwill. His work had only one goal – to undermine Western democracy.

Yes, Ivor Montagu, the godfather of Ping-Pong, had every reason to feel satisfied with all he had achieved.

Thanks to him, it had become all the rage in the US. And now he reasoned the game's popularity was strong enough that he could use it to spread communism around the world.

NINE

PLAYING POLITICS
(LONDON, 1950)

Montagu knew exactly who to address his letter to. Over the last decade, he had read and reread Edgar Snow's book, Red Star Over China, a sympathetic account of the communist revolution, complete with the interviews that glorified and glamorized the revolution's leaders Mao Zedong and Zhou Enlai. It was in this book that he learned of Zhu De, the founder of the Red Army, the honorary chairman of the Sports Commission and the man he needed to contact.

But with no response, Montagu became increasingly anxious and his panic attacks grew more frequent, becoming at times debilitating. And so, in a desperate attempt to get Zhu's attention, he wrote a pamphlet titled "East-West Sports Relations". In it, he made the implicit suggestion that table tennis could be used as the ideal tool to advance the communist revolution. And it worked.

Within only a month of the pamphlet's circulation,

Montagu was granted a visa to China as the British representative of the World Peace Council, a communist front that was popular amongst Western socialists. Montagu had no idea that Western democracies had also been watching him and had figured out the word "Peace" was simply a cover for "Communism".

In October of 1952, while the People's Republic of China celebrated its glorious third anniversary, Montagu found himself in the VIP section with the party's Central Committee standing near Chairman Mao and Zhou Enlai. Watching the massive crowd from the stands, he thought about how he had been responsible for China not only joining the International Table Tennis Federation (ITTF) but also ensuring that its membership be recognized as a national organization rather than a provincial one. It had taken some wrangling since Taiwan also wanted to join the ITTF, but China's claim over Taiwan's sovereignty created an obstacle. Predictably, the United States and Western democracies recognized Taiwan's independence, while Russia sided with China. This gave Montagu a chance to do Mao and Zhou a big political favor by stipulating that Taiwan could join only if it went by the name, "Taiwan Province of the People's Republic of China". Thanks to Montagu, the game of Ping-Pong was now officially being used as a political tool between the East and West.

Weeks later, in front of an enormous crowd at the All China Table Tennis Championships, Montagu proudly proclaimed that China would soon be competing with the rest of the world. He knew it was all a lie. The best players in China had no chance of winning on the world stage. But he also suspected that would soon change.

TEN

EMPTY STOMACHS

Chairman Mao had an hour to think about the political fallout he was facing before Premier Zhou Enlai was expected for a meeting. He knew he was facing widespread dissent, and he also knew Zhou would sugarcoat the truth in fear that he would take his anger out on him and any other party official who dared to tell him how catastrophic the Great Leap Forward had really been.

Were the people so naïve to think it was going to be easy? Did they not get that, in order to move forward, the country would need millions of people to work in the manufacturing sector? Did they not understand that the only way to get it done was to relocate men and women to the cities to work in steel mills and construction?

Furthermore, who the hell did they think would build the grand structures he envisioned for Communist China. Did they think these impressive structures that would ultimately symbolize the greatness of China build themselves? Were the people stupid or simply unin-formed?

But Mao was no fool. He could blame the people all he wanted. He knew the truth. The Great Leap Forward wasn't unfolding as he planned. The new state-run farming practices were a disaster. Planting crops too closely and plowing the land too deep had damaged thousands of acres and was producing far less than needed to feed the country. Millions were starving to death and getting sick from the barbaric approach to steel production that was polluting the water and soil. And so, by the time Zhou stood at the door, Mao had worked himself into a foul mood and let loose.

"Zhou, unless you have come here with a brilliant plan on how to feed millions of people, shut the fuck up."

Zhou's adrenaline raced as he followed Mao to the kitchen, who was screaming for his cook, Li Kun.

"I'm starving. Bring me lots of red braised pork, cabbage and wild vegetables and make it fast. Don't just stand there, you idiot!"

Li ran to the stove. He knew he was under time pressure but luckily today there were no surprises in Mao's order. Over the last few months, he had become well accustomed to Mao's eating habits that rarely strayed from Hunanese peasant food.

He had perfected all the rustic dishes and could now whip them up efficiently. Mao had made it very clear to him, and the many cooks who had come before, that he despised those who ate well to show off their wealth while others went hungry.

Grabbing the large pork shoulder, Li tried hard not to think of his parents who were starving. Mao's so-called disgust for those who ate well made him furious even though he had tried hard to rid himself of the deep resentment he harbored. He knew the only way to survive was to keep his anger buried. So, he heated the wok, chopped the pork, threw in some ginger, onion, soy sauce and garlic and then added a heaping spoon of salt. He hoped the extra sodium would make Mao's recent stomach aches worse – a whole lot worse. He was sick of hearing Mao's belching and farting and was willing to take the risk – willing to make Mao suffer for the hunger his parents endured.

Li served the steaming pork along with the cabbage and vegetables in separate serving bowls. He hid his smile behind a straight face while he watched Mao grab all the food for himself. Had Mao ever considered the needs of anyone else? Did all of the political bullshit that spewed from his mouth ever really have to do with the collective good of the people?

Li quietly walked back to the kitchen where he strained to listen to the conversation between the two leaders. He could tell by Mao's tone that he was angry and aggressively leading the discussion with Zhou, who was agreeing with every word.

"The pork is good. It's fine for us but we must remember to save some for our athletes. We must keep them strong. The others can survive on less."

Zhou nodded dutifully. Mao continued to rant.

"Our Ping-Pong stars must look strong like they've been well fed, well coached and well taken care of by the state. Do you understand?"

Zhou took a big gulp while Mao grabbed another large portion of meat and belched loudly before wolfing it down. Li reappeared and asked if everything had been to their liking and if they would like anything else.

"What do you think? We're greedy? No! We don't want any more. We're done! Now clear the plates and get me some tea and put some fresh ginger in it. Let it steep, I mean really steep. My stomach is still upset and it's not letting up."

When Mao finally finished slurping down the ginger tea, he got up and went to his office, followed by Zhou. The door closed behind them, and Li knew it was time for him to wash the last teacup and leave. Mao, laden with unrelenting paranoia, didn't like his workers hanging around if they didn't have a purpose. They were there to work and once their tasks were completed, they needed to get the hell out. If he thought a worker was listening to his conversations, they usually landed on a farm in the Hunan region doing unbearable manual labor.

It was cold outside. Li put his hands in his pockets to keep warm and found a coupon, a liáng piào.

He looked at it carefully and wondered how the small piece of paper would keep him, his wife and two kids alive for the next month. The government had introduced the coupons recently. The monthly ration of food was thirty-three pounds for men and twenty-eight pounds for women. There were no coupons for children. It was understood that parents would share their meagre rations. But most could barely survive on the allotments they were given, and many were forced to secretly find small pieces of land so they could grow their own food. If they were caught, they were usually shipped off to labor camps or publicly used as an example of being a traitor and tortured to death. A large piece of secret land signified a greedy comrade, the worst kind. Mao's government made it very clear on billboards and other propaganda that this behavior would not be tolerated. The people should consider themselves lucky and enjoy the plentiful food the government had made available to them.

Li carefully put the coupon back in his pocket. He knew it was imperative that he not lose or damage it. But he couldn't help but think of the two pounds of pork he had just prepared for one of Mao's meals and it made him angry once again. He considered for a moment ripping up his skimpy food ration in protest.

But his rebellious thoughts were interrupted when he noticed a woman who seemed to be watching him. Was she a spy? They were everywhere and spied on anyone who worked directly for Mao. No one was off limits. Li looked directly at the woman.

"What are you looking at, you stupid fool?"

The woman scurried away without making eye contact.

Feeling a little spooked, Li decided he would go early

the next morning to the government-run food warehouse and pick up his rations. He knew there would be no meat until Chinese New Year when households were allowed to slaughter one pig they had raised.

As far as Li was concerned, Mao was a pig.

ELEVEN

HUNGRY FOR VICTORY

Even the wretched smell couldn't keep the crowd away. They just kept pushing and cramming their way into a local fish market to place their bets on the scrawny, teenage Ping-Pong sensation, Rong Guotuan.

Rong's family had fled mainland China in the 1930s during the Japanese occupation hoping for a better life in Hong Kong. But the "better life" never came, and the family eventually put all their hopes into Rong who cleaned fish during the day and played Ping-Pong at night. Rong's boss, a practical man, promised him as long as he kept winning, he would ensure that he and his family would never go hungry. Rong figured it was a simple, straightforward way to keep his family going.

With every win, word of his prowess spread. It wasn't long before he was recruited to play for the prestigious Hong Kong team against the Japanese team in Tokyo. Rong could hardly believe that he, an eighteen-year-old nobody, would be facing the Japanese legend and world champion, Ogimura. And when the match was over and he had won two out of three games, it was hard to tell who was more surprised.

From that point on, Rong's life was never straightforward again. Weeks after his Tokyo win, Rong was invited to play an exhibition match in Beijing where he demolished his opponents. Although in the past his technique had sometimes been sloppy, these days his instincts kicked in and nobody could touch him.

Before returning home, he received a special invitation to lunch. He didn't know whether to be honored or frightened. His hosts were two of the most decorated generals in Mao's army and they wasted no time asking him if he would consider returning to China to play for the national team. He would be trained well, paid well and fed the tastiest and healthiest food in the country. Rong left lunch agreeing to consider the offer, knowing he had already made up his mind. He had no choice. Ping-Pong had become the only way to keep himself and his family alive.

Initially, Rong was apprehensive of what kind of reception he would receive. He had heard of the nine-month political reeducation many returning Chinese endured. But he was astonished at how well he was treated. In his mind, he was living the good life. Even when his tuberculosis returned, he was taken to the best sanitarium in the country to rest for six months with no questions asked or pressure put on him to get well faster.

In April 1959, having fully recovered and feeling strong again, Rong played for the Chinese team at the International Table Tennis Federation World Championship in Dortmund, Germany. China had never won a medal in any sport, anywhere. And Rong did not disappoint. He quickly made his way to the semi-finals where he crushed the American, Marty Grossman. In the finals, Rong faced the Hungarian champion, Ferenc Sidó, who was considered a beast. But Ferenc didn't stand a chance against Rong, who danced around the table, smacking the ball with remarkable ease, skill and power.

Now, Rong, China's first Ping-Pong champion, stood proudly to accept the trophy from none other than the Honorable Ivor Montagu.

That same day, Montagu gave another, more important, prize to the Chinese. He invited China to host the 1961 Table Tennis World Championship. It was two years away and, with his guidance, would give China enough time to develop a strong team and give him the perfect front he needed to spread his agenda.

TWELVE

THE PEOPLE, THE PLAYERS AND YELLOW GOATS

Zhuang Zedong felt weak. The measly portion of rice he ate daily was barely sustaining him anymore and he knew he would soon starve. The Great Leap Forward was killing people by the millions. There was barely any food left in the country. Even the black market had little to offer.

Over the last few years, the vast majority of wheat, corn, rice and beans had been exported for hard currency to pay off debts to Russia and to finance Mao's ambitious construction boom that included the largest Ping-Pong stadium in the world. Mao was determined to have China be a perfect showcase for the 1961 Table Tennis World Championships even if that meant sacrificing people.

Zhuang, always aware of conserving his energy, sat down and thought about how lucky he was compared to most. He had recently been told by an official from the department of physical education that if he continued to work hard, he might make it from the local sports school to the provincial team. He had heard that athletes who made it to that level were fed decent food. But Zhuang also knew that the competition to get there would be brutal.

Ping-Pong tables had been set up in barns, classrooms, stores, factories and even hospitals. The rapid pounding of the little white balls echoed through the countryside, towns and cities – day and night.

Hundreds of thousands of young Chinese, just like Zhuang, would be sent off to play in tournaments across the country. Any fear of being away from home was quickly squashed by fear of starvation at home.

Over the next year, not only did Zhuang make it to the provincial team but, in September of 1960, he was chosen as one of the 108 best players in China to be on the national team. There, he would have the good fortune to meet Rong, who befriended him quickly and made a big effort to show him the way things were done.

At times, both men could hardly believe the privilege that came with being a member of the team. There was new equipment, comfortable clothing and running shoes and the quantity and the quality of the food was something they had never experienced before. The generous rations included a breakfast of milk, sweet cakes, rice porridge, buns and pickled vegetables. Mao had gone so far as to station a shooting team in Inner Mongolia to hunt for yellow goats, a delicacy in China. He figured that way the team could eat meat for lunch and dinner. No matter what, he would ensure his athletes were well fed and in tip-top condition.

But all the privilege came at a price. As the Table Tennis World Championship approached, so did the physical and psychological demands on the players. The team was isolated in training camps far from towns and cities and the training schedule was often unbearable. Days were spent on forehand drives, backhand top spins, forehand top spins, serves and countless exercises to ensure players were swinging short and aiming low. That, along with endurance and weight training, was followed by incessant lectures on "psychological warfare".

And while the punishing regime was unrelenting, Zhuang and Rong reminded each other that there was no life for them back home. They had received word that both their families had perished, and they knew Ping-Pong was the only way to survive.

THIRTEEN

CRUSHING VICTORY (BEIJING, 1961)

"Our athletes are not here to entertain. They are here in solidarity… and to crush our enemies."

Chairman Mao

The opening ceremony was a two-hour spectacle of gymnastics, tumbling, dancing and fireworks. The extreme training the Chinese team had endured was about to be thrust onto the competition. The team had been told to obliterate their opponents. Anything less and they'd end up at a labor camp where they'd eventually starve to death.

The Ping-Pong superstars who came from around the world were totally unprepared for the powerful force that was about to be unleashed on them. The Chinese team first defeated their Cuban comrades with little effort. The crowd cheered so loudly they were instructed by officials over the loudspeaker to tone it down and cheer equally so as not to appear inhospitable.

Next, teams from New Zealand, Poland and England were brought down relatively quickly which left them shell-shocked and asking their coaches how the hell it happened.

And finally, the match for the men's gold was up between China and Japan. The Japanese had already won five straight championships and were counting on a sixth to make it a world's record.

For the Chinese, the match was critical. It was revenge for the humiliation China had suffered under the years of Japanese occupation. Every stroke would be payback for the Nanjing Massacre and the mass rape, torture and murder that left Chinese heads and bodies strewn on the streets. Nothing less than the honor of China was at stake.

Rong was up first. The players could barely hear the ball over the screaming home crowd. But soon, the Chinese fans fell silent. They were in shock. The Japanese had won.

Now China's hopes were placed on Zhuang who would face the Japanese superstar, Ogimura. At this point, Zhuang was fit and fearless and every bit as fast as his legendary opponent but with the extra advantage of being seven years younger.

The stadium shook from the excitement. The players found it hard to concentrate over the deafening roar. The Japanese coaches complained but the pleas for quiet over the loudspeakers were ignored. In the third tie-breaking game, Zhuang charged ahead, taking the lead and winning 21-13, a humiliating score for the Japanese. Thanks to Zhuang, China had just become the world champion.

In the excitement, Chairman Mao stood up on the raised platform and waved. The crowd went wild with a standing ovation that went on and on while Ivor Montagu, standing only a few feet away, applauded and smiled broadly as he looked around at the packed stadium full of China's elite.

And while the thrill of victory was almost deafening inside, hundreds of starving peasants quietly rifled through the garbage bins at the rear of the stadium in hopes of finding a scrap of food.

PART THREE

THE GAME

1949-2023

FOURTEEN

KINDRED SPIRITS
(OHIO, 1949)

Miriam and Hildi were late for the bus. Panicked, Miriam grabbed her favorite paddle, a handful of balls and the newspaper lying on the coffee table. She screamed at Hildi to hurry up. Hildi was running late again. She had come home past midnight from one of her many dates. Miriam never quite understood all the time and effort Hildi devoted to that part of her life. Her clothes, her hair, her desire for a family – all the things Miriam didn't care a rat's ass about. For her, the world of Ping-Pong was enough.

The bus station was three blocks from their house. Luckily, they were both fast runners. They would get there just in time. Stumbling into their seats, they knew they had two and a half hours before arriving in Toledo where they were scheduled to play in the National Women's Doubles tournament.

Hildi grabbed the small pillow from her bag, nestled it

against the bus window and closed her eyes. Miriam gave her a gentle nudge so she could spread out her newspaper, but when Hildi didn't budge, she pushed her a lot harder. She was sick of Hildi's reckless behavior and lackadaisical attitude towards Ping-Pong. It was as if she had no clue how talented she was and how far she could go if only she'd put in more effort and be more disciplined. Hildi needed a kick in the ass. She needed to stop thinking about finding a husband and concentrate more on the game.

The Stahl sisters were starting to be recognized as superstars in the slowly expanding world of Ping-Pong, and Miriam knew it was no time to take her foot off the gas. She loved it when people referred to her as Miss Ping. She considered it a name that reflected her hard work and dedication to the game. Hildi, on the other hand, vehemently discouraged everyone from calling her Miss Pong, as tempting as it was. To her, it sounded ridiculous, and she worried that it could hinder her social life.

But other than their views on men, marriage and Ping-Pong, Miriam and Hildi were deeply connected. They had the same strong body, the same open heart and the same sharp mind.

Miriam opened The New York Times. Her eyes widened. The headline read: "Fall of Mainland China to Communism. Mao Zedong declares the creation of the People's Republic of China".

Miriam had heard about communism from her mother as if it was pornography and from her history professor who positioned it as a political bonanza. The two accounts were so different, she decided to try to sort it out for herself. She read on. She wondered about the idea of everyone being considered equal... no rich... no poor... no one being jealous because there was nothing to be jealous of. Miriam thought it sounded a bit strange, having lived all her life in Columbus, Ohio where the rich kids lived up on Signal Hill, the poor near the tracks and the middle, like her, lived downtown. She hated the way everyone had been slotted and the unfair symbols of wealth. Was communism really possible? While the bus rocked back and forth, Miriam thought how this controversial movement might actually make sense.

She put the newspaper down. She wanted to think more deeply about it, but her mind quickly wandered to Ping-Pong, the way it almost always did... back and forth... from the piercing sound when her paddle smashed the ball to the pure exhilaration she felt while playing. She wondered whether Ping-Pong was sort of like communism. It didn't discriminate. There were Ping-Pong dances, Ping-Pong picnics and Ping-Pong parties where everyone was invited. It really was a game for the people, the same way the communists referred to the people, the People's Republic of China.

FIFTEEN

THE PLAYERS
(USA, 1960)

Jack Elliott put down the phone. His stomach felt queasy. Now the Department of Sport and Recreation was questioning him about his players and quietly threatening to withdraw funding if they didn't provide the American taxpayers with sporting entertainment that was exciting and dynamic. How had the simple game of Ping-Pong, the one he loved and had devoted much of his life to, become so complicated? As the coach of the US team, he knew exactly what he was doing. From determining the best model of approved Ping-Pong paddles to the most effective exercises to keep his players strong and agile, he had put together the strongest team in the world. There was one win after another. Up until now.

He reviewed the team in his mind and decided that the next time the government called he'd be ready to fight back. He would describe each player in infinite detail –

their stats, what they looked like, where they came from –
and he would be sure to add star quality even if he had to
stretch the truth. The world of sporting entertainment
liked that – the Hollywood stuff, the sexy stuff, the pizazz.

He sat down at his desk and opened a file titled,
"Dietary Recommendations for Elite Athletes" just as
Ricky Epstein stumbled into his office, holding a
notebook and looking nervously at Jack. Jack chuckled.

"Ricky, you're an educated guy. McCarthyism died
over a decade ago, right? Then why is our stupid
government making accusations that the game of Ping-
Pong is not dynamic enough for the television audience,
and why do they keep threatening to cut our funding? Or
is it because of our loss in Beijing and they're scared the
Chinese have finally built a team to rival ours?"

Ricky stared blankly at Jack as he continued to rant.

"I'll tell you what I think. It has nothing to do with the
loss of viewership and everything to do with there being
so many Jews on the team. The government still thinks
that all the Jews in this country are communists."

Jack looked at Ricky and burst out laughing. Ricky
looked confused.

"You're a Jew, aren't you, Ricky?"

Jack knew he was making Ricky, his new twenty-six-year-old hire, squirm, but he didn't care. Ricky was his fourth hire that year. Jack had impulsively fired the others, calling them "morons" and "complete duds". As far as Jack was concerned, if Ricky was going to survive in this job, he had to be quick and responsive to all of Jack's demands. Jack could be impossible, and that had become clear to Ricky soon after he took the job.

"So, Ricky, are you a communist? Are you planning to overthrow the government? Don't take this the wrong way but, so far, you can barely manage my coffee order, let alone overthrow the government."

Jack got up and pointed to the photos of the team members tacked on the wall. "Look at Jimmy McConnell. He's kind of a pain in the ass. He's cocky and obnoxiously arrogant with the spectators and the media. Technically, he's certainly not our best. As much as I've worked with him, his backhand drive is still weak. But he's wickedly intense and can stare down most opponents in no time. He's a real fighter. So, I guess we need to keep him.

"Now here's Marty Grossman. Just look at him. He insists on wearing those stupid, thick, black-rimmed glasses, which the camera really doesn't like. I keep telling him to get contacts, but he ignores me. He tells me his glasses give him a 'distinctive look'. Oh ya, undeniably distinctive. He looks like a Jew. He never listens to what I have to say. He never listens to what anyone says except for Miriam, but I kinda think he has a thing for her. He's impossible most of the time. I'm no shrink, but I have a hunch it has to do with that overbearing mother of his. She's impossible. Did you know she calls me three times a week to remind me that her darling son 'needs to be on a very specific diet'? She refers to him as a 'superstar athlete' and then goes on and on about how critical it is that he has four ounces of protein twice a day to ensure his muscles stay strong. That woman is a major pain in the ass just like her son. Christ!"

Jack stopped ranting for a bit and looked out the window.

"Anyway, as much as I'd love to get rid of him, I can't. He can smash that fucking ball like a missile. You just know it's not coming back. We absolutely need to keep him. He's the best player we have, maybe will ever have."

Jack then stared at the two pictures side by side.

"Had you started working for me when the Stahl sisters played New York? They were unbelievable. The crowd went wild. Miriam is a lot more aggressive and a lot more intense than Hildi. Her forehand topspin is the best I've ever seen. And even though Hildi is probably just as talented, her weapon isn't her natural ability as a player. It's simply that she always looks like she's having a blast on the court and she's a real piece of ass. The audience adores her. Can you imagine if Hildi wasn't a beauty and looked more like Miriam? Those girls would probably get a fraction of the coverage they enjoy today. It's interesting. I don't think Miriam gives a crap about what she looks like. She's a real tomboy. Ping-Pong is what makes her tick. Did you know the media has started calling her Miss Ping?"

Ricky looked distraught at Jack's crude assessment of the Stahl sisters.

"Grow up, Ricky. Looks and labels count, especially now with the government up my ass about pizazz."

Jack sat back down and glared at Ricky.

"So, Ricky, I'll tell you why the Department of Sports and Recreation is really up my ass. It's Marty and the Stahl sisters. They're Jews and the government is scared of the optics, so they cover up their anti-Semitism by complaining about the ratings. They're such idiots."

The conversation had clearly taken a turn that Ricky wasn't quite prepared for, but he knew he needed to push back. Ricky had only worked as Jack's assistant for two months but was already tired of his rants and cocky know-it-all management style. So, he decided to launch a counter-attack.

"Jack, do you know why there are so many Jewish Ping-Pong players around the world?"

Jack was stunned by Ricky's brazen tone and chose not to respond. He would test Ricky to see if he had the balls to stand up to him.

"After the war, when the Jewish immigrants were settling throughout the US, they were still suffering from the aftershock. You can understand why, right, Jack?"

Jack looked at Ricky as if to say, "Are you fucking kidding me?" But Ricky wasn't done and took a big breath to steady himself.

"Parents were scared. They were scared of many things, including sports that could hurt their children. They needed to keep their kids safe. Have you ever noticed how few Jewish football, soccer or hockey players there are?"

Ricky knew he had taken a big risk, but he wasn't

backing down now. "You see, Jack, there was little risk with Ping-Pong. The worst that could happen was a ball to the eye or a paddle chop. Furthermore, unlike many sports of the time, it didn't exclude people. Everyone could play. That's the reason why today there is an unusually high number of Jews in the sport."

Jack fixed his eyes on Ricky. "Get me a coffee. I take two sugars, not one, you idiot."

SIXTEEN

THE DIRT
(ARIZONA, 2023)

Jenny glared at her mother.

"Mom, what the fuck. I already see Grandma once a week. Isn't that enough? What do you want from me?"

Ronnie took a deep breath. Her emotional fortitude was completely spent, and she had no energy left to nuance a toned-down response.

"You know, Jenny, your grandmother has always been good to you. Frankly, you've been acting like a two-year-old by blaming her for what's happening in your life when she really has nothing to do with it. Nothing! All she did was love the game of Ping-Pong and she worked bloody hard at it to become a superstar. Yup, that is her crime.

"Furthermore, have you ever considered that your grandmother is getting older and slowing down? Who knows how long she'll be around. Jesus, Jenny, maybe you might just consider thinking about someone other than yourself for just one second and grow the hell up!"

Jenny, shocked by her mother's angry response and weary of her own inner rebellion, reluctantly agreed to go.

Ronnie went upstairs to call her mother. She needed to warn her that the visit could be rocky. Miriam listened carefully and immediately called Hildi to come over. She was considered the light and easy one and good at diluting tense situations. Now, armed with backup, Miriam didn't flinch when the doorbell rang.

"Oh, Jenny, I'm so happy to see you. Come in, come in. Just watch you don't trip over all the Ping-Pong stuff on the floor. It's been a nightmare working with the ITTF."

Hildi smiled and gave Jenny a hug. "Oh, Jenny, it's good to see you."

Jenny normally felt repulsed by any form of adult affection but figured it was easier to submit to her great-auntie rather than make a big show, especially after her mother's rant. When Hildi finally let Jenny loose, she quickly diverted her attention in fear of another hug.

"Grams, it looks like a bomb went off in here."

Miriam, holding a large tray of coffee, mugs and a plate of fruit, chose to ignore her granddaughter's comment.

"My doctor told me my days of cupcakes and cookies are over. My sugars are up." Ronnie looked tense.

"You didn't tell me that, Mom."

Miriam chuckled. "I purposely don't tell you this stuff 'cause I know you'll make a big fuss."

Jenny grabbed some grapes and started to survey the Ping-Pong paraphernalia. Making her way through the mess, she stumbled on an old Dunlop Maxply wooden tennis racquet.

"So, Grams, what's with the tennis racquet? I thought you were the Ping-Pong Queen."

Ronnie could hear the sarcasm in Jenny's voice and shut her eyes. Miriam caught the tone.

"Yup, I played some tennis."

"Were you any good? I mean, why would anyone give up tennis to play Ping-Pong?"

Hildi, abruptly, interrupted. "You know, Jenny, I don't think your grandmother really wants to talk about it right now. It was a long time ago."

Miriam took a slow sip of coffee. Actually, she did want to talk about it. She had wanted to talk about it for a long time. "Was I good at tennis? Damn right I was!"

Jenny detected a tone in her grandmother's voice that she had never heard before.

"When I was in the ninth grade, I played varsity on my high school team. Number one singles. The senior girls were not happy because I beat them all. Then I beat all the girls in the county. Then I beat all the girls in the state. And when there weren't any more girls to beat, I started to play against the boys. And I beat them too. And your Auntie Hildi was not far behind."

Miriam took a deep breath and crossed her arms. "But some of the mothers on the boys' teams took offence that their darling sons were having to compete against us, so they complained, citing the so-called 'inappropriate' nature of mixing the sexes in competitive sports. They made up some garbage about rules and codes and regulations. And so, we were asked to leave."

Miriam got up and rifled through a stack of papers on the floor. She handed Jenny a newspaper clipping from the Columbus Free Press with the headline, "Stahl Sisters Get Kicked Off the Boys' Varsity Team".

"That was the official story. The real one was hidden behind the insidious anti-Semitism at the time. Remember this was the forties and mothers weren't about to sit back and have two Jewish girls beat their darling Waspy sons. So they made our lives miserable, and within a few months, the only place we could play was at a court across town in a Jewish neighborhood because all the other courts in Columbus were so-called 'full'."

Miriam looked at Hildi.

"And so, we switched to Ping-Pong. At the time, it saved us. There were no restrictions. There was nothing stuck-up about it. It really was a game for everyone."

The room went quiet. Jenny looked at her phone in a desperate attempt to ward off the anxiety she felt creeping in. Ronnie, unable to hear the story again, picked up the tray and darted to the kitchen.

Miriam didn't give a shit. She actually felt relieved. For almost all her life, she had presented herself as an intense, confident athlete. But now, in her later years, the wounds were oozing, and she no longer wanted to cover them up the way she always had. She knew her years were numbered, and it was time for her granddaughter to hear the truth. She also knew it was time for Miss Ping to tell the real story of the drugs, the politics and the Chinese players whose lives were sacrificed.

After several minutes, Hildi broke the silence. "You know, we were so goddamned good, we could have been as successful as the Williams sisters."

SEVENTEEN

MAO
(BEIJING, 1969)

Mao was frustrated. He was sick of China being patronized as Russia's communist sidekick. And to make things worse, his army had just killed over thirty Russian soldiers in a skirmish at the border. The incident was blowing up fast, and Mao worried that war could break out if he didn't manage the situation. He needed a political distraction.

For a moment, he questioned whether reaching out to the US as a potentially lucrative trading partner might be viewed favorably. But he immediately dismissed the idea.

Just thinking about those fucking American imperialists made his stomach turn.

Nixon (Washington, 1969)

Nixon blamed China for his dwindling popularity. China had screwed the US by siding with the North Vietnamese.

What the hell was Mao thinking sending all those arms, men and supplies there? Did he not have enough to worry about, having just starved millions of his own people? As he wiped the sweat from his forehead, he knew his anger was getting the better of him, and he knew he had to think strategically about his next political windfall. But instead of calming down, he panicked more. Where the hell was it going to come from?

EIGHTEEN

ON EDGE
(NAGOYA, 1971)

Miriam woke abruptly when the plane landed in Nagoya, Japan for the thirty-first World Table Tennis Championships. She was exhausted from the long flight and the rigorous training schedule Jack insisted they all follow. Everything was prescribed – wake-up times, diet, strength and eye-hand exercises, uniform regulations and pre- and post-game analysis.

Miriam was still pissed with how Jack had grabbed her arm at the airport before they boarded and handed her a red cosmetic bag full of make-up.

"Listen. I know nothing about this shit except I've been told that the camera likes red lips and big eyelashes. Miriam, there will be lots of cameras."

Furious, she had pitched the bag in the nearest garbage. She would listen to Jack on all things related to Ping-Pong, and that was it. How she looked was none of his fucking business.

When the plane finally arrived at the gate, Jack blew his whistle and immediately started barking orders. Miriam took a deep breath and whispered in Hildi's ear, "I'd like to strangle Jack with that whistle right now. Oh God... I'm exhausted."

Hildi grinned and gently steered Miriam to get in line behind the rest of the team. Jack just kept yelling about how to wear the uniform properly and how to greet the Japanese officials who were waiting on the tarmac.

"Don't forget to bow at a thirty-degree angle and say konnichiwa properly. Please pronounce it correctly so you don't sound like idiots, and whatever you do, don't look away. It's considered a real insult."

Ricky squeezed past the players, rummaging through a bag to ensure that all the paddles, balls and official team paraphernalia were there. He had been told that under no circumstances was that bag to be checked with the rest of the luggage. Ricky knew if anything went missing, Jack would fire him on the spot. He was itching to find the smallest reason.

After the greetings were over, the team was ushered onto a bus and taken to the Kyoya Ryiut Hotel. They had a few hours to rest and prepare for the next game. The bus would be leaving for the sports stadium at 2:00 sharp, and no one would be allowed on unless they had showered and were wearing a clean uniform. Jack looked very serious while he delivered his message.

Marty Grossman looked over his glasses and imitated Jack's expression. Jack caught it and shot back. "Hey, smart-ass… I know you think you're indispensable. But, just so you know, you're not!"

Nagoya Sports Stadium

The US team walked into the Nagoya Sports Stadium at exactly 2:30. Jack led the way while Ricky brought up the rear holding the precious bag. It was eerily quiet.

The stands were already full of spectators speaking in hushed tones, nodding politely and smiling at one another. Hildi thought she heard a man from midway up the crowd say, "Fucking Americans", but she wasn't positive.

Stunned, she pulled Miriam aside. "Did you hear that?"

Miriam shook her head. "Nope."

Miriam had heard it but was trying hard to stay

focused. She had ten minutes to prepare. She needed to zone in on her strokes, her technique and her plan of attack rather than some wingnut who hated Americans.

Jack barged into the women's locker room looking for her. It frustrated the female athletes the way he did that. They had complained to him on several occasions. But this time, they gave him a pass since his voice was tense and the stains under his pits were embarrassingly visible. They knew he couldn't have cared less where he was. He just wanted to find Miriam before she was up.

"Listen, Miriam, or should I say Miss Ping, you're a crowd-pleaser. Give the audience what they want, what they came for. Now, your opponent is aggressive and has been known to play dirty. Tire her out, make her sweat and bring her down."

Miriam stood in the wings, listening to the loud applause when Toshika Kayama walked on the stage. She couldn't help but notice how much the applause dwindled when the host finally motioned her to go.

Toshika steadied the ball on the palm of her free hand before launching a heavy topspin shot directly at Miriam who drove it back with as light a topspin as she could to produce a low ball. Toshika kept driving the ball to the right, then the left harder and harder. Miriam consistently volleyed back, defensively controlling her shots. She wanted to keep the ball low. She could block it better that way.

She was aware of conserving her energy and not draining it too early, especially playing against Toshika who was much younger. Back and forth… back and forth… ping, pong, ping, pong. It was hard going. Toshika's serves became increasingly more aggressive. She was now smashing the balls continuously to the left to put them away. She had obviously studied Miriam's moves and had identified her weaker side.

But Miriam strategically kept the ball low and blocked the shots coming at her one after another… consistently… methodically. Miriam figured it was the only way she had to combat Toshika's aggressive plays. She had to tire her out, move by move, stroke by stroke… ping, pong, ping, pong.

After an hour, Miriam noticed the intensity of Toshika's shots was weakening. And Miriam knew it was time. Time to muster what energy she had left and smash the balls back, fast and hard. Miriam's unexpected assault took Toshika by surprise. She was too tired to defend

Miriam's attack that lasted ten minutes. Miriam's strategy worked and she won the match. Now in her mid-forties, she felt completely drained. But she knew she still had it as she walked off the stage, smiling and waving politely to the crowd. Yes, that was the way it was done. Yes, that was why she was called Miss Ping.

Jack ran after Miriam into the locker room to cheers of delight. Miriam thought it was funny to watch Jack, oblivious to his surroundings. Miriam jokingly punched his upper arm.

"What are you doing in here, Jack? Does it say, 'All Are Welcome' on the door?"

Jack stopped and grinned. "Relax, I came in here to tell you how amazing you were out there. My God, that was a well-executed game. You controlled every second of it. Congratulations, Miss Ping!"

"Thanks, Jack. Now can you leave?"

"Yeah, yeah, I can. But hurry. The men are up next, and Marty is playing. It's going to be a wicked game."

Jack was right. It was a wicked game, with Marty's opponent smashing balls in his face, trying to take out his eyes. It was a dirty trick that Marty had seen before. But it didn't deter him. Marty slammed the balls back like missiles, the way he was famous for. And the balls didn't come back. They bounced hard on the floor… boing, boing, boing… until a referee ran to pick them up. Not surprisingly, the game didn't last for long, and not surprisingly, Marty won. The US Ping-Pong team was successful once again. After the tournament was over and the US team shook hands with their opponents, as was customary, the athletes headed to the locker rooms.

The Wrong Bus

After his win, Marty, as usual, spent too long in the shower and didn't make it onto the shuttle bus back to the hotel. Jack was pissed and had told the driver to go ahead. The idiot could figure out how to get back on his own.

Unfazed, Marty found a guy, who he thought was from the Japanese team, to play a pickup game. He wasn't that tired and wanted to practice his topspin. The game was intense from the first serve and Marty, thrilled by the strength of his opponent, had to work hard to keep up. But once again, Marty's natural ability enabled him to smash the ball with remarkable skill and speed, and in no time, he won hands down. Feeling particularly self-satisfied, Marty followed his opponent out of the Nagoya Sports Stadium and stepped onto the only shuttle bus left in the parking lot.

The Chinese players were dumbfounded when Marty climbed aboard. They had never seen a capitalist pig close-up before, let alone one with a dopey smile and a bad haircut. Marty, sensing the hostility, started backing up when Zhuang got up from the back of the bus and walked towards him, extending his hand. Relieved, Marty smiled and shook Zhuang's outstretched hand with gusto. Inspired by Marty's openness, Zhuang then grabbed his gym bag and, to the astonishment of his team members, presented Marty with a silk-screen portrait of the Huangshan mountains he had received from a fan.

Knowing he needed to reciprocate somehow, Marty clumsily rummaged through his bag and pulled out a comb. Looking at the partially toothless offering, he frantically dug through his bag again and pulled out an old, worn T-shirt with the words "Let It Be" emblazoned across the front. It was the best he could do.

Little did he know that his smelly and somewhat torn T-shirt would be the catalyst for a geopolitical pivot that was exactly what Mao and Nixon had been so desperately looking for.

The international journalists, who had been lucky enough to follow Marty getting on the Chinese bus, went wild. They immediately swarmed Marty and Zhuang who, by this point, were posing together like old pals. Flashbulbs popped while the journalists scribbled furiously. When Marty was asked if he'd like to visit China someday, he laughed and pulled Zhuang closer.

"Yeah, that would be cool! Very, very cool!"

NINETEEN

THE BROWN MANILA ENVELOPE (JAPAN AND WASHINGTON, 1971)

Feeling lousy having downed nine celebratory glasses of champagne the night before, Jack could hardly focus on the brown manila envelope Ricky had placed in front of him. He managed to tear one end, revealing a thick piece of white paper with a red ribbon tied around it. It was an invitation to the US team for an all-expense-paid visit to the People's Republic of China. The top of the invitation read, "Friendship First, Competition Second". Jack was stunned and needed a few moments. No, a few moments weren't enough... he needed a few hours.

He needed to think, to organize his thoughts and to call Washington for advice. The response from the State Department was clear.

"Don't do a goddamn thing until you hear back from us."

And in less than an hour, the phone rang and a senior official gave Jack his instructions in no uncertain terms.

"President Nixon has made it very clear that the US can simply not 'afford to leave China outside the family of nations', and if Ping-Pong is the way to do it, so be it. Do you understand, Jack?"

Jack understood.

The second he put down the phone, he screamed at Ricky to assemble the team before dashing to the meeting room.

"Do you understand what this means? Nobody has been invited to that country since 1949. This is fucking huge! We only have a few days to pull it together and to make our team perfect, not just to show how good we are at Ping-Pong but also to show the world that we are number one in every way and plan to stay that way. And if you don't think this is a big deal, think again. Time magazine has already got hold of this information and plans to feature the story as 'The Ping Heard Around the World' for their next issue."

Marty shook his head and imitated Jack's expressions. But Jack caught it from the corner of his eye and let his pent-up anxiety loose.

"Smarten up, you wise-ass Jew!"

Everyone was startled by Jack's overreaction. Marty

sat down, took off his glasses and glared at Jack. He knew he was the team's strongest player and didn't appreciate being reamed out in front of the team. But Jack, completely overwhelmed by the crushing pressure he was now under, continued to rant.

"You know, Marty, you're a cocky little shit. You think you know it all. But getting on that bus being all cool and kumbaya-ish was naïve and asinine. You got in way over your head on this one, big man. And now, I have to clean up your fucking mess!"

Miriam and Hildi sat at the back of the room taking it all in. They couldn't believe what they had just heard. Jack could be incredibly harsh, but they had never heard him speak that way. Maybe being at the center of this political stage was too much for him. Maybe the game had outgrown him.

TWENTY

THE RED, WHITE AND BLUE ENVELOPE (ARIZONA, 2023)

Ronnie looked at Jenny's bedroom, took a deep breath and knocked gently on the door.

"What do you want?" Jenny snapped.

Ronnie froze.

"Mom, you were just here. You're hovering again. I'm fine."

Ronnie steadied herself, entered the room and handed Jenny an envelope just as Becca poked her head in the door.

"Really, Mom? Whatever is in here, I really don't want it. And get out, Becca! Mom came in to see me, not you!"

Once again, Ronnie felt caught. She was well aware that Becca had been fending for herself over the last few months, and it left her feeling guilty and inadequate as a mom – a feeling she had struggled with since becoming one.

"Jenny, stop it. Becca doesn't deserve that. Becca, can I talk to you in a minute? I won't be long."

Ronnie turned to Jenny who had ripped open the envelope and was glaring at the invitation.

"I really hope you'll reconsider going to Grandma's big day. I won't ask again."

Ronnie knew she didn't have the energy to wage battle with Jenny yet again, so she left the room. She had said enough, probably too much over the last few weeks. With more, the backlash could be unbearable.

Almost immediately, Jenny crumpled up the invitation, threw it on the floor and frantically texted Dimitri about how much she "hated fucking Ping-Pong" and how her mother was making her "insane".

Dimitri told her to meet him at the parking lot behind the pool.

TWENTY-ONE

THE CALL
(JAPAN, 1971)

Ricky ran to answer the phone on Jack's desk, spilling coffee along the way. He groaned, knowing Jack would be pissed when he saw the brown splotches on his desk.

"This is the office of the president. President Nixon would like to have a word with Jack. Is he available?"

Ricky panicked. Jack was not available. His binge drinking and junk food were resulting in longer and more frequent visits to the bathroom. Judging by the time, Ricky figured Jack was probably in mid-purge.

"I'm terribly sorry, but Jack is on the court with two of the coaches watching the players practice their topspin."

Ricky wondered about what could happen to people who lie to the President of the United States and felt ill.

"Have him call this number as soon as he returns." Ricky nervously scribbled the number down and said goodbye.

Nixon sat in the Oval Office reflecting on how he had spent the last two decades publicly denouncing communism. It was an evil system. Mao had essentially locked up the entire country by shutting it off from the world and starving millions of people along the way. Most of all, he hated how Mao had supported North Vietnam in a war that seemed like it would never end and was responsible for weakening his own country's economy and reputation. The divisions at home were deepening, and he feared that the country was losing its international prestige. He knew the American people were longing for peace at almost any price. Something had to be done. He had publicly announced on several occasions that the true strength and power of a leader lay "in his ability to give history a nudge". And he knew that at this point, with little else to hang onto, Ping-Pong was the only conduit he had to make that nudge happen.

And just as his thoughts wandered away from China to how his political adversaries were pushing domestic issues like highways and education, the phone rang.

"Mr. President, it's Jack Elliott on the line, sir."

"Put him through."

"Good morning, Jack. Tell me about the status of our Ping-Pong team."

"Good morning, Mr. President, sir. I think we are in good shape for the upcoming tournament in China, sir."

Nixon paused. "Tell me about this Marty Grossman that I've been hearing so much about. I understand he's a superstar on the court but a bit of a loose cannon. Is that true?"

"Well, sir, you are right. Nobody can return a smash from Marty."

Nixon continued. "That's not what I'm asking. Jack, how are you managing him? We cannot have another incident like the one when he wondered onto the Chinese bus and acted like an idiot. I heard he offered the Chinese player a dirty black comb with teeth missing and then a fucking old Beatles T-shirt. Jesus, Jack! He made us look second rate.

"Listen, let me be perfectly clear. Now, more than any other time, America can never, ever look second rate to the world."

Nixon purposely paused for a good long time to make Jack sweat, a skill he had perfected while in the White House.

"Jack, let me put it even more simply. Players like Marty, as talented as they are, cannot jeopardize our success. I cleaned up the goddamned mess he started on the bus, but I won't clean up another."

"I understand, sir."

Nixon figured he had bullied Jack enough and had gotten his message across, so he backed off. His tone softened.

"Jack, do our players have absolutely everything they need?"

"Yes, sir, they do."

"Okay then. Let me know if you need anything. Bye, Jack."

"Goodbye, Mr. President."

Jack put down the phone and ran to the bathroom. The conversation had left him feeling nauseated. But his mounting anger quickly overcame his urge to vomit, and he began to yell.

"Ricky, where the hell are you? Get in here."

Ricky got up slowly from the small desk the Japanese officials had brought in for him to use. He no longer jumped quite so fast to Jack's orders, and his adrenaline no longer spiked when he heard his voice. Ricky had convinced himself that his nightly reading of The Calm Soul was providing him with enough peace to manage Jack's abuse.

"Where the hell is Marty?"

"I'm not sure, sir."

"Well, find him now."

Ricky left Jack's office and made a few calls.

He returned an hour later with Marty unshaven and reeking of body odor. "Hey, Jack. What's up?"

"Don't fucking 'hey' me, you idiot. You stink."

Marty wasn't surprised by Jack's aggressive attack. He was used to it by now.

"Why are you more miserable than normal, Jack?"

Marty reveled in his clever, smart-ass comments and worked hard delivering them for maximum impact. Between that and his natural athleticism, he figured no one could penetrate him.

"Well, Marty, let me explain why. I just got off the phone with President Nixon. Yes, President Nixon, and he told me how unimpressed he was by your dumb-ass move. He said, and let me quote, 'I heard he offered the Chinese player a dirty black comb with teeth missing and then a fucking old Beatles T-shirt... he made us look second rate and, let me perfectly clear, America can never, ever look second rate'."

 Marty stood there feeling uneasy.

Jack continued berating him. "So, Marty, if you don't follow the rules, or if you take one, just one, misstep, you'll be out on your ass. Your hairy, cocky ass. Do you get it, Marty?"

For the first time, Marty, who had lived and breathed Ping-Pong for most of his young life, felt threatened. How did stepping onto the Chinese bus and pulling out his comb become the business of the President of the United States? How was this happening?

"I get it, Jack."

TWENTY-TWO

THE TRIP
(JAPAN, 1971)

The next few days were brutal. Washington flew in three officials from the State Department to "help the players fully understand the importance and complexities of their upcoming trip". They were told that Nixon expected them to play with grace and humility. They were also told that the training would be intense, that there would be nothing left to chance and there could be absolutely no missteps to threaten this political opportunity for the US.

All players were required to be in the gym at dawn for strength and aerobic training, followed by two hours of strategy and technique. They were given a half-hour for breakfast, after which they attended eight hours of training in Mandarin and cultural norms, punctuated only by a short lunch.

More drills and game strategy followed until dinner at 7:30, after which the players dropped from exhaustion in their bed. There was no time for touring or fun. There was barely time to breathe.

The officials reminded Jack repeatedly that his role was to help manage and support his players through the rigorous training. The team was required to follow the schedule to the minute, and there could be absolutely no deviations.

Jack found these working conditions at times unbearable and directed his anger and frustration directly at Ricky.

"Ricky, I told you the team only gets thirty minutes for lunch, not forty! Those morons need as much time in the classroom as possible, so we don't have a screw-up. Do you think you can get it right? Jesus, I don't know why I just don't fire you now. Fuck! I guess at this point, I couldn't bear to break in another idiot."

As Jack's abuse became almost unbearable, Ricky considered quitting several times. But every time he came close, he backed down. He wasn't prepared to forgo seeing the politicization of Ping-Pong unfold in front of his eyes. He had a front-row seat, so for now, he would take it.

Hildi acted like a good little soldier and did exactly as

she was told. For her, the highlight was the language lessons. She loved playing around with all the new words she was learning in Mandarin. And when her teammates got sick of listening to her and told her to "shut up" or worse, she'd completely ignore them and make up something silly.

"Ping-Pong and ni hao,

"Learn it 'cause of Chairman Mao."

Miriam found it annoying that Hildi seemed to be managing it all with ease. At times, Miriam found the schedule agonizing, and there was a point in every day when she thought of quitting. But instead, she lashed out at Hildi – the safest punching bag she had and one sure not to punch back.

Everyone could see that Marty, the laid-back Californian and vocal advocate of peace, love and drugs, was struggling the most. He looked pale and thin and had little to do with anyone – except Miriam, the woman he deeply respected and the one he had spent several nights with over the years.

At times, Miriam found watching Marty wither in front of her eyes unbearable and grew increasingly resentful of Jack pounding him non-stop.

On the fourth day, Jack told the team they had the evening off and made a big deal about what a good guy he was to be giving the players free time. Being a good guy had nothing to do with it. His nausea had become worse and, at times, he felt like he could hardly breathe under the crushing pressure.

As soon as Marty heard the news, he bolted out of the hotel and made a beeline to a secret, abandoned train station on the southern limits of Nagoya. Over the last few days, Marty had made friends with the concierge who told him he could get what he needed there.

When Marty stepped into the station, he was approached by a young man carrying a small brown bag. As he got closer, he couldn't help noticing how rough the man looked. His skin was sallow; his eyes had sunk; and he stank of old sweat and weed. His pupils were dilated and darting back and forth, and he seemed on the alert for anyone who might spot the hand-off. The man held out the bag and, in remarkably good English, whispered, "Hurry up... here it is. Give me the money."

Marty knew he had to move fast so he grabbed the bag, glanced inside, reached deep in his pocket and handed over a wad of sweaty cash. The man took off before counting it partly because he was too agitated and high to focus and probably needed the cash for his next hit.

Marty stuffed the paper bag into his jacket and took off back to the hotel. He gingerly took a few crystals from the vile inside the bag, crushed them with the bottom of a drinking glass from the bathroom and carefully placed the white dust under his tongue. Marty knew the drill. So, he laid on the bed and waited. Within an hour, he became obsessed with the new paddles Jack had forced him to play with. They were moving, swirling and turning all around him.

Jack's voice boomed in his head and his words echoed.

"Marty, look at these new paddles we just got in. These are going to be our greatest weapon. You'll see. You'll be able to smash balls faster than you could ever imagine. You'll demolish anyone who tries to bring you down."

But Marty hated the new paddles. He was convinced they were heavier and more cumbersome than the old ones. He thought his serves were off by a millisecond and backspin was slow. The new paddles were making him feel increasingly anxious. He pleaded with Jack to get the old ones back, but Jack refused.

His hallucinations took a dark turn when Marty thought Jack was a monster and was trying to kill him. He saw himself in a dark, empty stadium, standing at one end of a Ping-Pong table with Jack's shadow facing him at the other end, smashing balls made of lead in his face.

Marty's enhanced state was making him sweat and his heart race. He fought to remember how much acid he had taken, but he couldn't, and in a moment of panic, he thought he was going insane... one crushed crystal at a time.

The next half-hour was filled with panic. Images of Jack smashing balls at his head, Miriam attacking him with a paddle over and over and Ricky leaning over his body mumbling words from the Torah left him completely overwhelmed. Marty lay there, his body curled into a ball, his legs tucked under for protection against his enemies. He was paralyzed with fear.

As the hours passed, Marty tried desperately to release the terror in his mind. He tried to focus on the mechanics of the game, the back and forth, the sound of the ping, the serve, the smash and the absolute rush he felt when he played.

And finally, the terror gave way to a sense of delight and mental clarity. He could now play the perfect game; every shot, every backspin and every chop was precise and on point. No one could come close to his moves. And soon, any feelings of fear or doubt had completely dissolved into intense excitement and joy. It felt overwhelming, almost too much, but he wanted it to last longer, maybe even forever.

In the middle of the night, Marty knew his trip was ending when his feelings of all-encompassing joy started to fade; the beautiful geometric patterns he saw on the Ping-Pong tables dwindled; and the balls were no longer sky blue. He felt reluctant to go back to his normal consciousness and had a strong urge to freeze his mind exactly where it was.

But he knew he had to pull himself together. Ping-Pong was his life, and the trip to China was critical. He knew he had to perform and be his best self. He also knew if he took one misstep, Jack would get rid of him.

TWENTY-THREE

THE LITTLE RED BOOK (BEIJING, 1971)

"Communism is not love. Communism is a hammer which we use to crush the enemy."

Chairman Mao

Mao sat quietly poring over the report from the Ministry of Culture and Sport about the Ping-Pong tournament in Nagoya. He thought about the Americans winning every game and became agitated when he read about Marty getting on the wrong bus and talking to his athletes for all the world to see. If anyone was going control how relations might unfold between China and the US, it wasn't going to be from some American kid who was espousing peace and love. He rang a bell and a young beauty walked through the door and stood at attention waiting for orders.

"Yes, Chairman Mao."

He smiled slyly while he examined her perfectly

balanced face and lean, delicate body, while he thought about what he could do with her. Being somewhat insecure of his own appearance and the ugliness of his aging wife, he almost resented her natural femininity and beauty.

"I need to speak to the General of Culture and Sport."

"Is that Xiu Peng, sir?" the beauty replied.

Normally he would have torn shreds off a secretary who didn't know that information inside out, but he was craving her, so he held himself back and replied gently, "Yes, it is. Please get him on the phone immediately."

She smiled slightly more than was necessary, but she knew her future depended on playing the game.

Five minutes later, the phone rang on Mao's desk and General Xiu Peng was on the line.

"General, I'm reading the report you wrote about the performance in Nagoya, and I'm not pleased. Can you explain why our players are coming second? Can you explain how that stupid American found his way onto our bus? Can you explain why that was seen all over the world? Do you realize all the time and effort I spent turning this global embarrassment to our advantage?"

There was silence on the other end.

"We can never, let me repeat, never let the Americans show superiority over us. Is that clear?"

"Yes, sir," the general stuttered.

"The Americans are coming here in a few days. Now what are you planning to do to ensure our players win?"

"Sir, we have our athletes practicing fifteen hours a day. Their technique is being analyzed carefully and we recently replaced two players with, I believe, stronger ones."

"My dear comrade. If they're playing fifteen hours a day non-stop, have you not thought that they might be tired? They need to rest, you idiot! And I assume they're getting enough protein? Fuck! They better be since I practically have a full army hunting for those bloody yellow Mongolian goats."

There was more silence.

"Thinking clearly is imperative for athletes. Have you considered that? Do they rest their minds enough?"

"Yes, sir. We have thirty minutes of meditation scheduled every day."

"Hmmm. Xiu, have you read my Little Red Book?"

"Yes, sir, of course I have."

"What can you quote from it that will help our athletes perform better?"

Xiu tried to quiet his mind. He knew of those who had been put to death for misquoting Mao's words. He took a deep breath and slowly spoke, desperately trying to get each word right.

"We think too small, like the frog at the bottom of the well. He thinks the sky is only as big as the top of the well. If he surfaced, he would have an entirely different view."

"So, Xiu, I'm happy you know that. But I guess it's time for you to get your head out of the bottom of the well. The world will be watching us. There is no room for losers, including you. Do you understand what I'm saying?"

Xiu was shaking on the other end of the line. He felt hot and dizzy and didn't know how much longer he could endure Mao's wrath.

Mao didn't say another word for several seconds before slamming down the phone.

He then rang the bell again and the beauty appeared by his side.

"Make me a cup of tea with lots of ginger and meet me in the next room."

The beauty ran off to the kitchen, her cheeks flaming red as she frantically asked Li, the cook, to prepare the tea. Slowly, she knocked on the adjoining room to Mao's office with the trembling tray of tea in hand. She knew exactly what was expected of her.

TWENTY-FOUR

MARTY'S BACKPACK
(NAGOYA, 1971)

Marty was jolted awake by the sound of the alarm and he felt like hell. He shook the contents of his backpack onto the bathroom floor, searching madly for the aspirin bottle to calm his pounding head. When he spotted the infamous comb, he grabbed it and broke it into dozens of pieces before downing two pills and standing under a hot shower, trying desperately to wash off his hangover and Jack's abuse.

He grabbed his clothes, tossed his paddle into his backpack and hailed a cab to the gym. When he marched onto the court, Jimmy McConnell, Marty's nemesis on the team, looked amused.

"Hey, Marty. What's going on? You're on time."

Marty shot back. "Oh, fuck off! I'm here alright. You wanna play a round?"

Jimmy, being somewhat surprised by the offer, agreed once he had finished his topspin drills. Twenty minutes later, they faced off. Marty took immediate control. The anger that had been brewing inside of him took over every serve, smash and topspin.

Marty's shots were flawless and seemed effortless. Slowly, the other team members gathered round to watch. It was a match like they had never seen before. One by one, the balls flew by Jimmy. Sweating profusely, he tried every trick and gathered every bit of strength he had, but Marty was unstoppable. Hildi looked on in disbelief at the speed of Marty's moves and remarkable power. Miriam kept her eyes not so much on the game but on Marty's face. How it looked thinner and how his usual cocky grin was no longer there. She knew the drugs were keeping his nerves in check for now, but it was a quick fix that would come to bite him.

After the game, Jimmy, dripping wet, walked slowly to the locker room. Marty stood there looking blankly at the court.

Miriam pulled up two chairs.

Marty barely looked at her. He was trying hard not to. He knew their age difference was an issue and had been told by Jack that having a relationship with her would fuck up his entire career. But no matter what Jack had to say, he would always have time for her and what she had to say. After all, she had thrived in the world of Ping-Pong for several decades, and Marty knew it was no small feat athletically or emotionally.

"That was something like I've never seen from you. Your moves were perfect. I don't know how anyone could top that. But, Marty, you look thin and worn. You okay?"

"Jack's up my ass. Big time."

"I know."

"No, you don't. Nixon called him on it. The President of the United States, for fuck's sake. Jack told me that if I don't win every single game and 'behave myself', I'll be out on my ass. My 'hairy, cocky ass' to be exact."

Miriam looked at Marty, trying hard to understand why Jack was taking such a hard line.

Marty grabbed Miriam's arm to anchor himself.

"Ping-Pong is my life. It's been my whole life since I was eight when my dad walked out on us. It saved me. It's what I do. It's what I know. If Jack takes it away now..." He looked desperate. "I dunno what I'll do."

Knowing there was a lot hinging on her next comment and desperate to find the right words to console him, she decided a platitude was the best she could do in that moment, knowing it was safe.

"Listen, Marty, tomorrow is a new day."

She knew it was a dumb thing to say, but she needed time to think it through. Marty had been very naïve marching onto the Chinese bus and attracting all that attention.

Jack was right. He had no clue about the world outside of Ping-Pong, and his ignorance had caught up with him.

Marty stood up and gave Miriam a blank look.

"See ya later. I've got to take a shower."

TWENTY-FIVE

JENNY'S BACKPACK
(ARIZONA, 2023)

Jenny threw her backpack over her shoulder and ran out the door. She had been texting with Dimitri and was now late for her appointment with Dr. Salter. As difficult as these sessions could be, she never missed one. She thought of them as a secret hiding place where she could question and evaluate her "shitty life". She could say anything. There was never any judgment, and Jenny enjoyed the mental and emotional freedom that came with these sessions.

"My parents won't stop bugging me about Grandma's event – the big fucking reveal of Miss Ping for all the world to see. Honestly, I don't think too many people are going to give a shit what my grandmother did in the seventies."

Dr. Salter smiled, thinking to himself how the teenage mind could be simultaneously so simplistic, yet complicated. He reasoned that was why so many of them were messed up, having to deal with these competing forces.

"Have you given any thought to why your mother is making such a big deal about it?"

Jenny snapped back. "Did you forget who you're talking to? Since I quit school, I have lots of time to think about this shit. It's kinda what I do. Mom says I ruminate too much. What a stupid fucking word. Thank God I have Dimitri to talk to. He gets me, you know."

"Well, do you? Do you ruminate too much?"

"Probably, but I need to. I need time to think about the fucked-up shit that's happened, and if I don't, I find my thoughts melt together and my anxiety becomes unbearable. To be honest, the only person I feel calm around these days is Dimitri."

"Jenny, can we circle back to why you think your mother is putting so much importance on your grandmother's big event?"

Jenny saw a message on her phone, grabbed it and looked at the screen. It was Dimitri. Dr. Salter looked agitated.

"Jenny, c'mon, you know the rules."

"Fuck... okay. Here's my take. Being Jewish back then

wasn't exactly easy, and I think Ping-Pong let my grandma escape from the anti-Jewish bullshit and nasty bullying that was all around her. So, when my mother was born, I don't think Grandma really knew what to do with her. Maybe even Mom was an annoying distraction. Mom once let it slip that Grandpa was the one that raised her, and so when he died, she felt completely lost."

"And what does this have to do with your mother making such a big deal about you not going?"

"It's simple. Mom has always felt second rate to her mother. She thinks Grandma's real love has always been Ping-Pong, while Grandpa and she didn't even come a close second. Mom's a big pleaser. Ever since Grandpa died, she's been busting her butt to please Grandma. At times it's pathetic to watch."

"So, do you feel bad for your mother?"

"Sometimes I do. And sometimes I ask myself why I don't just suck it up and go. Dimitri knows the whole story and tells me not to become a pleaser like Mom or I'll hate myself. Fuck! Doesn't he know by now that I already do?"

Jenny put down her head and paused.

"You know the saddest part of all of it? Grandma

taught us how to play Ping-Pong, and Mom and Becca are okay, but it's so obvious that I'm by far the strongest player in our family. I can smash those little balls faster and with more control than Mom and Becca could ever dream of. It feels natural to me, and I know Grandma has always loved playing with me more than Mom or Becca. The whole thing makes me feel guilty. Fuck!"

Dr. Salter followed her to the door. "It's complicated."

"It sure fucking is." Jenny looked desperate. "I just don't know."

Dr. Salter dreaded comments like that from his patients. They were hard to respond to and, with his next patient waiting, he knew he needed to find a few words to quickly wrap up the session. He felt pressure to pass on something for her to think about before their next session.

"Just remember, tomorrow is another day."

He knew it was a dumb-ass platitude and was angry that he couldn't do better than that.

Jenny grabbed her backpack, plucked out a chunk of hair from the back of her neck and slammed the door.

TWENTY-SIX

LOSING IS WINNING (BEIJING, 1971)

The American team was physically and mentally exhausted from their "day off" touring the Great Wall and Tiananmen Square. Walking miles up and down stairs in the bitter cold had been uncomfortable. Even their faces hurt from constantly smiling in front of their hosts, the international press and the American diplomats who came along to monitor the team. One wrong comment or gesture of any kind and they'd be escorted back to the hotel where they would receive yet another lecture on cultural norms.

Fortunately, the day went off without incident and the team was relieved to be back at the hotel, relaxing in the lounge set up exclusively for them. Finally, they could take a breath before tomorrow's exhibition game.

Jack walked in, looking even more anxious than normal. Maybe it had something to do with the man tagging along behind him.

Miriam knew something was up. "Hi, Jack. What's going on?"

Jack ignored her.

"Okay, everyone, listen up. You all know how much is riding on tomorrow. The world will be watching. America will be watching. President Nixon will be watching."

Marty couldn't believe that Jack had the balls to give them another speech on the importance of winning. Jesus Christ, he thought. Fucking enough already.

"In fact, the president himself has given me firm instructions. Tomorrow, you will use all your athletic talent and ability..." Jack paused, "...to let the Chinese win."

After a long, awkward pause of deafening silence, Marty couldn't hold back. "Are you fucking serious?"

"Ya, I am fucking serious," Jack shot back.

"You especially have no idea what's at stake here. You need to let the Chinese win. And you better not make it look obvious either. It's a matter of national security."

"Fuck! Tricky Dick is screwing us," Marty said under his breath but making sure it was just loud enough for everyone to hear.

"Hey, you'll show respect for the President of the

United States, young man," the man behind Jack screamed.

"Oh, sorry. I meant to say fucking Tricky Richard."

The Chinese Team

The athletes sat courtside in the world's largest Ping-Pong stadium waiting for their coach to deliver his usual pep talk. But when they saw who he was with, they immediately stood up and bowed.

"Please sit, comrades," said Xiu Peng, the General of Culture and Sport.

"I come to you with direct orders from our great leader. Tomorrow, Chairman Mao will be watching carefully, and in his infinite wisdom, he has decided that you will permit the Americans to win. Winning will give them a false sense of superiority which we will use to our advantage."

The team listened in silence. Zhuang knew the drill better than anyone. The winners had often been decided beforehand. But considering the international attention on tomorrow's event, even he was a bit surprised.

"Listen to me. Tomorrow, you will not be great

athletes. You will be great soldiers. Your weapons will be your paddles and your skilled deception. By permitting the Yankee oppressors to win this one battle, we will win the greater war and bring honor and glory to the motherland and to our great father."

The team, taking a cue from their coach, stood up and burst into applause. They had no other choice.

The Match

After the elaborate opening ceremony at the People's Sports Stadium, Marty and Zhuang were up. They began by hitting hard, but without the usual degree of power or spin. The crowd couldn't tell the players were holding back, but Marty and Zhuang sure could. Something was off.

Over the years, Zhuang had become a master at throwing games and did his best to set up his opponent for killer returns. Instead of going for the corners as he famously did in international play, he would aim a few inches inside to give Marty a better angle. But Marty's returns came right back to Zhuang who wondered what the hell was going on.

Back and forth they went. Ping, pong, ping, pong. Marty tried his best but ultimately Zhuang was the true master of manipulation and skillfully lost the first game out of three. He could hit long and wide and with perfect accuracy. Looking over at Jack's angry face, Marty knew he had to lose the second game. Fortunately for him, he did. Now with the score tied at 1-1, they both knew they needed all the skill and talent they possessed to lose the third and final game.

At 5-5, Marty, about to serve, looked directly at Zhuang's face, whose expression immediately changed. The journalists and spectators who noticed thought the athletes were engaging in psychological warfare.

And just as Marty stepped forward to serve, he nodded slightly. Only Zhuang detected it and completely understood. From now on they'd be playing to win. Fuck politics.

The last few minutes of the game were intense. Zhuang kept smashing balls a few millimeters inside the left edge of the table that Marty, feeling physically and emotionally spent, couldn't return. The final game went to Zhang who walked off the court with his head down.

The rest of the afternoon unfolded with the players from both teams skillfully manipulating their scores and wondering what the hell was going on with their opponents. Miriam, feeling completely discouraged after deftly losing her game, couldn't stop thinking about how the simple game of Ping-Pong had become so politicized and corrupted.

Montagu, who had been seated directly behind Mao, was sickened by the display of deceit he was witnessing. He had watched every play carefully and realized his lifelong dream to control the spread of communism through Ping-Pong was over. It was no longer in his hands. Now he was the manipulated one.

Jack was relieved that Marty did as he was told, or so he thought. Nixon would finally get what he wanted. His "brilliant" plan would give history the nudge the US so desperately needed.

Mao understood that Zhuang had tried his best to lose. The American was simply too incompetent. He reasoned there was nothing he could have done playing against the American moron without making himself appear as a second-rate athlete and a disgrace to his country.

At the end, after the athletes had shaken hands, Mao stood up to a raucous crowd. He smiled and waved while congratulating himself on his brilliant strategy. Now the

Chinese could finally face the Americans on a level playing field.

133

TWENTY-SEVEN

JENNY
(ARIZONA, 2023)

Jenny felt relieved to be alone in the house at last. The fight that ensued had exhausted her. She needed some quiet after Ronnie's rampage.

Jenny felt proud of herself for shooting back at her mother and telling her the truth. She was sick and tired of being forced to live in a family defined by her grandmother's Ping-Pong legacy. Why couldn't her mother accept the reality that Ping-Pong had taken a heavy toll on her life, on her grandmother's life and countless others.

And in the quiet of the living room, Jenny realized that by refusing to go, and refusing to play the game again, her fight was over. She would no longer need to push back against the false narrative that her mother had created.

Exhausted, Jenny threw herself on the sofa, texted Dimitri to come over and turned on the sports channel just in time to see Iga Swiatek hit an impossible two-handed backhand winner down the line.

TWENTY-EIGHT

THE INDUCTION CEREMONY (ARIZONA, 2023)

Miriam felt uneasy getting dressed in the navy pantsuit and black pumps Hildi had insisted she wear. Ronnie and the family would be there in ten minutes to pick her up.

She didn't say a word when she got into the car. Nor did anyone else. Jenny had made her choice.

The large wall facing the entrance was covered with photos of Miriam smiling and shaking hands with Montagu, Nixon and even Mao. On the left, there were pictures of her goofing around with Hildi, Jack and Marty, and tucked in the corner, there was a black-and-white photo of Toshika nailing a topspin with Miriam looking exasperated.

To the right, there were articles from Time magazine and the Chicago Times that were prominently featured among the letters from the US Table Tennis Association and the Department of Health and Physical Education.

Even the poem, "Pingpongitis", had been hung on the wall. Closest to the door stood Miriam's trophies lined up like soldiers and miraculously not broken from Marc's recklessness.

Marc greeted them with his usual big voice, patted Miriam on the back like a dog and grabbed her arm to show off what he had done. He blithered on about how much time he put into the photo gallery and got almost giddy over the dessert table.

"Look, Miriam. I found a special bakery that shaped all the cookies into paddles, and look at this amazing cake. It must have taken them hours to get the dimensions of the Ping-Pong table just right. And take a good look at the net. It's made of marzipan! We should take a picture of you beside it before you start devouring a big piece of it!"

Marc burst out laughing.

"We know how much you love sweets."

Annoyed as hell by Marc's tone, Miriam was about to let him have it when the executive officer of the USATT announced to the crowd how honored he was to be "celebrating the remarkable career of Miriam Stahl", and she knew it was time to shift into high gear. She smiled and waved to the crowd in exactly the same way she been instructed to before going to China.

Walking onto the stage, she glanced down at the three-minute speech Marc had meticulously written for her, paused and, in probably the biggest fuck-you moment of her life, began reciting "Pingpongitis" in a bold, steady voice.

Ping-Pong, Ping-Pong,
Such a silly, little game,
Play it tipsy,
Play it straight,
The results are all the same.

Boys can play, girls can play,
Nobody gets in a snit,
You can use a brush to bat the ball,
Just have fun,
Keep going,
Don't quit!

So pick up a paddle and a ball,
Or even a paintbrush will do,
Just bat it around and jump up and down,

Here's to pinging,
And ponging,
And YOU!

She knew it was trite and a backhanded slap to the time and money that the USATT had invested in the event. But she didn't give a shit. This was payback for all the times Marc had patronized her as an old woman, how anti-Semitism got in the way of her playing tennis, how Jack insisted she wear mascara and lipstick for the cameras and for the enormous price the US and Chinese players had paid for having to swim in the political cesspool that Nixon and Mao had created.

When it was over, Marc was nowhere to be found. The crowd applauded politely, most of them convinced that Miriam had gone dotty in her advanced years.

ABOUT THE AUTHORS

LISA LUCAS

Lisa started writing for magazines and newspapers. Later, she wrote extensively on issues related to literacy and health that were featured in publications by the Canadian Public Health Association, several literacy organizations, and hospitals across Canada.

She is the recipient of the CIBC Children's Miracle Maker Award for advancing literacy among people with special needs. Several years ago, Lisa partnered with Laurie Stein and began writing for children covering subjects from climate change to refugees.

Her belief that "storytellers often sugarcoat real issues and present subjects to kids that are too far from reality in order to protect them. Just tell it the way it is. Kids appreciate authentic stories that are honest and real."

More recently, Lisa has turned her attention to poetry and historical fiction. *Ping* is her first novel. Lisa's work has been recognized by The New York Times, Kirkus

Reviews (starred), Publishers Weekly, Indigo and more.

Her books have been translated into several languages and are widely recognized throughout Canada, the U.S. and Europe.

STEVE LANDSBERG

Steve Landsberg, an accomplished, award-winning advertising executive and entrepreneur, is currently Co-Founder and Chief Creative Officer of Human Intelligence (H.I.), a New York City-based marketing firm. Prior to H.I., he co-founded *Grok*, an Inc. 500 "Fastest Growing Company."

Steve has held executive creative roles at many top global ad agencies leading the work on iconic global brands. A copywriter by trade, Steve has published numerous ad industry articles. *Ping* is his first published book.

www.historiumpress.com